The Invalid Citizen

and Other Stories

The Invalid Citizen and Other Stories

Short Stories

Gift Foraine Amukoyo

Soft Grid Limited

1

Gift Foraine Amukoyo

Published by

Soft Grid Limited

Plot 6, Block 23, Satellite Town

Calabar, Cross River, Nigeria

+234 (0)8027676550, +234 (0)8053110637

E-mail: softgridbooks@gmail.com

softgridltd@hotmail.com

www.softgridbookslimited.com

© Gift Foraine Amukoyo

First Published in 2018

ISBN 978-978-56095-6-1

Soft Grid Books

First Printing, December 2018

For my grandma,

Esther Willie Awerije

CONTENTS

One

Mira Won

I scrawled my signature on the first page of the document and paused. The pen slipped off my sweaty fingers. It was not easy for me to put an end to one's life.

Mira stared at me. Her eyes were remote, "If you truly love me, just sign it. You are the only family I have to permit this hospital to end these sufferings," she said.

"How can I? I do not want to lose my only family. You are the only one I have in this world."

"I cannot stay this way. I am troubling you."

"Stay with me. I do not mind. Stay as long as you can. I do not want to be your murderer. I will not be a party to this."

"It is not murder. It is suicide. I am killing myself. Do it, Tejiri."

"I will not let you do this. Mira stay with me," I held her pale fingers.

"Tejiri, you do not have a choice. Everybody will die one day. I am just going to die today."

"No Mira, I do have a choice."

"You should choose a sensible choice. Do it, and get back to your life. I am killing you with my illness. Tejiri, look at you. You are losing weight. I look chubbier than you are."

I laughed. "You wish, you wish Mira," I held her thin wrist, "yes, you look healthier than I am. That is why you should come home and take care of me. I miss all your soups and snacks. I wish a miracle could happen."

"I would have been rid of this illness a long time ago if it exists. All the fruitless dry fasts, vigils and prayers on the mountain showed I am unlucky to get healing. Miracle does not exist. If it does, then its healing hands have forsaken me. Oh, the wonders of heaven and earth, I need a healthy second chance to breathe without fear it might be my last. The thought of leaving you is the only thing that scares me." Mira turned her face away to hide the tears rolling down her cheeks.

"Mira, I am so scared of being without you. I will be so alone." I cried.

Mira wiped her tears and turned to face me. She sniffed, "stop crying like a little boy. You are now a full-grown man. Those manhood balls and beards are not for fancy. Tejiri, do not be careless. You resigned from your job to care for me. I have asked your boss to withhold your resignation letter. He did a dying woman a favour, and gave you leave for a week. You have five days left. Tejiri, sign those papers and get back to living your life."

Mira coughed blood for ten minutes. The sight was unbearable. I saw sorrows in her eyes and something mixed with an urgent plea. I picked up the pen and scribbled my final signature. A haughty nurse took the document away. Her smile and gait was triumphant. The near outcome of my action distorted my mind.

The doctor and two nurses returned with a lethal injection, "this would be fast. It is painless," the doctor said.

I could not witness Mira's death. I walked out of the room, thinking if my final decision was right. It had been unbearable to watch her suffer day and night. Mira's belly pain, unswerving nausea, and vomiting had left a painful twist in my heart. The cancer punctured holes in her intestines. Mira fed through pipes, she excreted on the bed. Sometimes, when the waste welled up in her bowel, the feces passed through her mouth, nose, and anus at the same time.

Mira's illness irritated some of the nurses. They were reluctant to attend her room. Once, I had heard a nurse gossip that I had lost my sense. *'He is swelling with her sickness. How can one person comfortably breathe in this foul corpse?'*

Mira had been my guardian angel. She was the shield that protected me after I lost my parents. I was fifteen year old. They died while protesting unpaid salaries and arrears. According to police report, stray bullets killed them. They were the backbone of the solidarity protest in Lagos. I had overhead Mira telling a colleague my parents were victims of a conspiracy.

My parents died as poor medical practitioners. Their professional and personal oath was to save life. They paid the hospital bills of strangers. After my parents' burial, none of their relatives was willing to be my guardian. They learned my parents' private hospital was bankrupt. Mira adopted me. She was a matron in their hospital.

I was weary. I shut my eyes. My head ached. It pounded to hear the confirmation on Mira's death. I did not hear any footstep towards me until a hand touched me.

"Tejiri, we won. The Judge has granted you permission to take Mira home until she passes," Kome said.

This news from Kome, my barrister gave me joy. I shed tears and hugged him tight. I ran towards Mira's ward. I called out to the doctor to stop the procedure.

I was panting by the time I reached the room, "stop doctor, your hospital has lost. You and your entire management have lost. I have won the case to take my Mira home. She is coming home with me."

My lawyer came forward with the injunction letter, "please, release the patient to my client. Henceforth, he is her caregiver."

My smile was radiant on hearing that statement, "yes, give my Mira to me. I know you all must have told her despicable things to make her hate herself and sought death as succour," I touched Mira's cheek.

She smiled weakly, "you are a fool. Oh, Tejiri, this is a foolish move. The stench will be so offensive in your home. After I am gone, the apartment will ooze for a long time."

"Yes, Mira, that is what I want. I want your fragrance to linger forever," the nurses' faces hardened as they cleaned up Mira, "hey nurses, I know none of you want to do this. Shed these long faces, do it with some smile. This is Mira's final departure from your hospital. I will take my Mira to an island. It would be Mira and me in paradise."

"I cannot wait to see this paradise," Mira said.

"It is just a small beautiful house on an island in Epe. Oh, Mira, you will love it."

✱ ✱ ✱ ✱ ✱ ✱

We were at the balcony. The morning sun cascaded upon us. The sun was like a healing balm. I was very cold last night; the mild heat soothed my skin. Mira felt at home. She was on a stretcher bed. I propped some pillows to support her back and arms.

"Tejiri, you are the greatest caregiver. I promise, I will not trouble you."

She looked fragile. Most of her hair was gone. Her eyes were the colours of a green river, dull and sad. I could not see the happiness her face used to exude. I opened a bar of chocolate and took a bite.

"Tejiri please let me have some."

"Mira, you are diabetic. This is sugary."

She scoffed, "Tejiri, Tejiri, can a dead body die?"

"No way, I am sorry. You can have this Mira and the rest in the fridge."

I opened the chocolate wrap some more and gave to Mira. She ate the soft chocolate with relish. She smiled. She savoured the taste and took another bite.

"Mira, it is time for you to have your bath."

"Tejiri let me be. I love it here," Mira snuggled deeper into the soft bed.

"I knew you would love it here. I had always said I would build a personal island for you. I am sorry it came so late."

Mira sighed deeply, "Tejiri, you have done enough. I am so proud of you. You are now a successful Petroleum Engineer. Cheers to more wealth," she gave a tiny piece of chocolate to me.

I took it and ate. I faced the pacific view of the island. Gush of fresh wind fanned my face, "this wealth means nothing without you to enjoy it."

"Go, get those chocolates, I want to eat every bar you have in that fridge."

"Okay Mira, I will get the chocolates."

"I love you, Tejiri."

"Mira, you know I love you very much." I pecked her on the forehead.

My bladder was full. I went to the toilet. As I urinated, a cold breeze caressed my legs. I shivered at the sudden chill. I wondered where it came from because the toilet temperature was warm. I looked at the closed door and window. I shook my head, flushed the toilet, and washed my hands.

I took my time to unwrap all the chocolates in a tray and covered it with a cloth. On my way to the balcony, I kicked my foot and yowled. I injured my big toe. I ignored the pain and hurried to the balcony.

Mira was relaxed in a pleasant position. She had put a pillow under her feet. Chocolate smeared her lips. I smiled and put the tray on a table. I knelt in front of her. "Mira, here are many chocolates. You are going to have a feast!"

Mira was silent and motionless. I took her hand. Her body had grown cold. Her eyes remained open. I closed her eyelids and sniffed. Mira did not wait to say goodbye to me. Tears rolled down my cheeks.

Two

The Transitional Title

Jessa was born in Jagua. When the oldest man in the village died, he looked forward to ascending the position. He received shocking news from the coronation council, that Jagua was not his real origin. Hence, they could not crown him as the Okpako-eldest man in the village. His ancestors had been wanderers. Jagua was hospitable and they had settled in the community.

Jessa's first-born, Jaja, was very angry. He vowed to sue the community to court. He wanted to prove them wrong that his clan from the fourth generation were not outsiders.

Jaja argued that when an individual had stayed in a particular geographic territory for decades, they naturally become citizens of the state. Migrants were accepted and respected as communal citizens. They had equal advantages despite there was no legal documentation of their citizenship in the past. Jessa talked his son out of going to court.

However, Jaja was adamant and filed a case. He told his father that the public denouncement of their clan was deplorable, "Tomorrow, I will ask questions around the village." Jaja said. "I shall trace our root."

The next day, Jessa went for an evening stroll. Jaja was waiting in the living room when he returned. Jaja stood up and guided Jessa to a seat. He placed his father's walking stick against the wall.

"Where have you been?" Jaja asked. "You look exhausted. I will get a cup of water for you."

Jessa drank the water slowly and finished it. Jaja took the cup and put it on the table. "Thank you, my son. What did you find out? You stayed out too long." Jessa said and brought out his snuffbox. He put some of the powder in his nostrils. He sneezed and tweaked his nose.

"Father, I have traced our lineage to Ebito. It is four villages away from Jagua. That was where your great-grand father migrated. The people welcomed me warmly. Father, they recognized the birthmark on my cheek. They said your great-grand father had the same mark." Jessa nodded excitedly, "I will go and build a house, a new home for us," said Jaja.

Jessa was not happy about this news. He did not want to leave Jagua. This land has been his heritage, "why build a new house so soon?" Jessa worriedly asked. He took the cup and put it between his thighs.

Jaja saw his father was unhappy. "Father, why are you sad? You should be happy we have discovered our real identity. By leaving Jagua, I know we will lose many things-some properties and precious memories. I would love we stay back, but the community have ridiculed our family honour. Do not worry father. It is never too late to start afresh. The worst harm should have been we were not able to trace our hometown. The good thing is that our kin still reserved some portion of land for us in Ebito. I will leave for Ebito tonight. We have much work to do. I called my siblings on my way back from Ebito. They have sent money for the building materials." Jaja knelt in front of his father and touched his feet. Jessa patted his shoulder. Jaja took the cup to the kitchen and went to his room. Jessa looked grave.

In the morning, Jessa took a stroll around the village in brooding silence. He went to the riverside, where he had spent most of his time; swimming as a toddler, and fishing as an adult. The river was good to him. It was in its beautiful white sand he had found a large piece of diamond.

Jessa did not covet it for himself, the whole village benefited after he sold the diamond. He sent his children and other children of the community to school in the city. His children were doing well in their careers. Four of his children lived in Europe, only Jaja, based in Jang, a town after Jagua.

Jakpo, Jessa's bosom friend walked up to him, "I saw Jaja this morning. He told me everything. Jessa, why do you want to leave? The people of Jagua have not asked you to leave. Are you very sad you cannot be the Okpako? Jagua cannot confer the title on you. You are not a real citizen of Jagua, which is why you cannot be the eldest member of the community. This title is like kingship. Jagua cannot give this title to an outsider."

"No Jakpo, you are mistaken. This title is honorary to a man that has seen many years on earth and in a territory. This title is not a legacy within a royal household. It is a transitional title for the everyday man.

Any worthy individual can earn it. Do you know how many decades I have been in Jagua? I was born here. I am eighty-eight year old. It is a privilege, when the gods bless a man's black hair to become gray. You cannot melt diamonds into gold. I have earned this honour. The coronation council thinks they have snatched my joy, but they are wrong. It does not matter whether the community bestows the title on me or not, by nature I have earned this right." There was silence for a while.

Jakpo cleared his throat and chewed his brushing stick; he spat some particles and chewed the stick again. "I am next in line. The people of Jagua will crown me Okpako."

"Yes, congratulation, my good friend and may the blessings of your ancestors dwell with you. We never dragged fishes in the river. There were enough fishes for every fisherman or fisherwoman to catch. We will not fight over a title. I wish you all the best my friend."

"Jessa, you should not go, you are a great part of this kingdom. Your ancestors live here."

"My ancestors also dwell in Ebito. I will use my last days on earth to offer libation to my ancestors. I have not known them, let me go and worship them in Ebito. Jakpo, I must go. Let me go back to my root. I pray I have a pleasant homecoming. I am positive my own people will not weigh me with scornful scale. Who knows, my friend? The gods have given me a chance to reconcile with my root. My children's offspring will not be a lost generation. They will not face denial from family. I just wonder who revealed this knowledge after many decades. I never knew I was not from Jagua. Who knows my history more than me?" Jakpo looked away, "Jakpo, do you have any idea of who revealed I was not originally from Jagua?"

Jakpo laughed nervously, "No my friend, I have no idea who that person is," he said quickly. "I hope you change your mind about leaving. Jessa, your decision is wavy like this river. I know you want to stay in Jagua."

"My heart will always be with this river, this water has lived in my vein, let me test the water of my origination. If it were up to me, I will grow older and die in Jagua. My children want us to leave Jagua for good. I have to obey my children's requests. A man is not afraid to walk naked in his own house. Only a guest has to be cautious around the house. I have a line of guests in Jagua. Let me take them back home. My children will feel like total strangers when I am gone. What is the essence of lingering in Jagua when the people showed us our place is not here? The heritage I pride in is not my children's identity. Let me take them home so that they can wear their badge with pride."

Jakpo looked beyond the river with a feeling of nostalgia, "You remember how we chased a rabbit into its hole," he said.

"We sealed the hole. We went to fetch firewood in the forest with which to prepare the bush meat and we could not find our way back." Jessa said.

"We considered ourselves bush meats when that wolf charged at us," Jakpo said and laughed.

"We were lucky the hunter killed it before it mauled us," Jessa said and snorted.

The two old men laughed. They recalled memories of running around the community as little children. Their smiles faded as reality set in.

"The days are grey and harsh." Jakpo said. "I will miss you old friend. When you are gone, I will be so alone. These youngsters do not have time for old grumpy men. Who will keep me company?"

"Who will come to visit and take care of me if I stay? I will lose Jaja and my other children if I do not go to Ebito. They have made up their minds. They want to leave Jagua forever." Jessa carefully bent down and picked a pebble. He clasped it and felt the coldness of the stone.

Jakpo nodded, "You have a great son in that young man, Jaja. I wish one of mine came back home. Decades of memories will drown after your departure. Farewell my friend, see you on the other side."

"I will miss you. I cannot tell you how much, you cannot see how well, my eyes are too dry to cry," Jessa hiccupped. He wished Jakpo well and left him by the river.

"I wish you will change your mind and stay my friend. I did not know the situation would become this ugly. I just wanted what was rightfully mine," Jakpo wearily said after Jessa's vanishing figure.

Jessa walked back home. Some children came around to play with him and he shared money among them.

Before daylight, Jessa and Jaja were ready to leave for Ebito. Jessa looked at the direction of the stream with longing. He imagined himself and Jakpo walking down with their fishing tools.

"It is not easy to detach from these memories," Jessa looked sad.

"Come father, you have said enough goodbyes. We should leave before the sun set, the road is not friendly on rush hour."

"Yes, some roads do not recognize old wheels that have always travelled on it. It does not have preferential treatment. Let us leave. We are no longer welcome here."

Two weeks later, the village elders had a meeting and concluded to use Jessa's house as their new meeting venue. Jessa had bequeathed the house to them. On the day of Okpako Coronation, bulldozers arrived.

The vehicle operator's voice boomed from a loudspeaker, "Everybody in this building should come out. In the next thirty minutes, this house would go down. At the count of twenty-nine, we would move in." He started counting, "One, two, three, four…" On the nineteenth count, the building was empty. The bulldozer destroyed the house on Jaja's instruction.

The people watched with sad faces as some men moved in with sledgehammers to break down blocks. No structure or block remained erect. A trailer packed the mashed cement and drove away.

"This is an unfortunate event. How can we hold the coronation ceremony in this ruin? We have to look for another venue or fix a new date for the coronation," a young man said.

"But, where is Jakpo?" The Community Chief frantically asked.

"He has not showed up for the ceremony. Has he heard the news? This unfortunate incident will devastate him. His ceremony has come to ruin, it can no longer hold today," an elder said.

"Jakpo must have heard the news. He knows everything. Was he not the one that discovered Jessa was not a real citizen of Jagua? He knows everything. After this meeting, we will proceed to his house. We will pay him a visit," the Community Chief said.

They did not meet Jakpo in his house. They knew Jakpo was fond of the river and thought he might be there. On their way out of his compound, they met the little boy that takes care of him. The boy told them Jakpo had not been home since sunrise.

"That is a strange behaviour. Let us check if he is at the stream," the Community Chief said.

They came to the river and saw him. Jakpo's body was floating to the riverbank. They rushed into the water and dragged the body out. He was dead. They saw his pair of shoe, reading glasses and a book under his favourite tree. Jeesa and Jakpo had carved some trees and made rooted benches by the river. His pile of belongings laid on it. The little boy fell down and cried.

"I guess he committed suicide. Oh, the dark realm has cast evil eyes on Jagua. Today is a very dark day in our history. Who will wake us up from this Omen?" A woman lamented.

"Look at this, Chief," the little boy cleaned his tears with his arm and handed a note to the Community Chief.

"Where did you find this note?" The Community Chief astonishingly asked.

"Chief, what does the letter say?" The woman asked.

The Community Chief read the letter aloud, *'I cannot live with myself after betraying my best friend, Jessa. I am sorry my dearest friend. My great-grand father had told me about your history. I told the coronation council because of my self-indulgence to be the Okpako. It was a sin to be envious of your status. Please, forgive me. No one should weep for me. I have already wept for myself.* **Jakpo.** *'*

Because he committed suicide, the community did not hold a burial ceremony for Jakpo. Jakpo's children carried him to the evil forest. They dumped his body for the beast of the wild to bury in their stomachs.

Three

I Will Bury My Father

The village town hall filled with tensed people. Everybody seemed to be at each other's throats with imaginary weapons. A muscular young man rushed at Ovie. Ovie poised to catch his balled fist and succeeded in twisting it until an elder separated their duel. The irate youth groaned and sat on the floor with drooping arm.

Ovie grinned, "Look at the weaklings that want to contest my decision. I will throttle anyone that dares me."

An old man came forward. He stared hard at Ovie and shook his head. He looked downward for a moment, stamped his walking stick, and looked up to him again, "Ovie, you should know the least one of our vibrant youths has only acted in a flash to repel your foolish decision. I warn you, more will come at you. An Army will defend your father's right."

"Let me see you all try. I will bury my father in Apele. He will be in residence at his mansion and nobody can stop me." In affirmation to the zealous statement, Ovie hit his chest, his chest was vibrating as if he had chest tremor.

"We shall see. We will prepare for our relative's burial rites. Watch how the lamp will find its way out of the wilderness to his shepherd fold." The old man said. He took a white chalk from his breast pocket and drew a circle. He looked to the roof and incanted inaudible words. His male servant brought a sick looking white cock. The old man untied the chicken's legs and incanted psalms around the body. The cock danced within the circle and fled outside.

The villagers left the town hall and Ovie remained resolute in burying his father in town. It was a custom for sons and daughters to lay in final rest in Godere. However, this city-bred child argued that since not every child was born in the village, it was not mandatory they follow the rules of the villagers.

Ovie turned to his uncle, Mamus, "Please, tell me how our distinguished guests will put up in the village. There are no hotels. There is not a single guesthouse to give them the least comfort. Those ridiculous invisible insects almost bit me to death when I first came here to fix a date for my father's burial. I will give my father a top society burial. The ceremony will be in grand style. Uncle, what do you think?"

"Ovie, do you seek my honest counsel?" Ovie looked away, "I thought as much, and you already know my stance on this matter. If you had been responsible, you would have built an edifice in the village that will accommodate your high society friends. Do you know why the youths are doing this?"

"You can tell me. Not that it would make any sense," said Ovie.

Mamus shook his head, "I will tell you. Many industrious sons and daughters of Godere tend to build mansions in the city and not lay a house foundation in Godere. The youths passionately carry out this custom to compel people to build houses in their villages and build business industries that will enable the village develop into a town. Your father wished for a burial ground in his father's house, and as he wanted, we shall fulfill his wish. It was his desire. I guess comfort is not your only reason for these dreadful shows you are putting on. You talk like a king and act like an ordinary palace guard otherwise you can postpone your father's burial until you build a grand hotel or motel!" Ovie looked at his uncle with contempt and stormed out of the town hall.

On the day of the burial, the youths of Godere hired a lorry to Apele. Ovie had brought police to safeguard the corpse in the mortuary. The irate youths charmed the police officers and collected their guns. The force men were fixated while the youths entered the mortuary and carried the casket.

They put the coffin in a car and released the police officers from the spell. They gave the police officers heavy slaps on the cheeks and kicks on the buttocks.

"This is a fair warning never to intrude on the activities of Godere youths. We will spare your lives. It is the solemn day of our brother's funeral rite. Count one another lucky because our battle is not with you but with that misguided child of the deceased," said the youth leader. He made a threatening move and the police officers scampered out of his way.

The youths gave the police officers menacing look before they got into the vehicle. The police officers ran into different hideouts until they zoomed off.

The Police Inspector of the squad was new to the locale. His junior officers had resisted the task to guard the corpse but he had threatened them with their jobs.

"Oga, now you see what we had told you. Nobody messes with Godere youths," a Sergeant said. He saluted the Police Inspector. The Inspector wiped dotted sweat off his forehead.

In many disputes, that Godere community was involved peacekeepers did not interfere. Any Security Commander posted to the area always mounted pressure to get transfer. When situations went awry, it was not easy to restore peace in the community. The peacekeepers always stayed in the outskirt of the community. They feared the clash between communities could crush them overnight if they rested in their temporal quarters.

The youths drove to their relative's mansion in Apele. They disseminated tents, toppled chairs, and tables. Some of them carted away with the foods and drinks. The burial took place in Godere.

Ovie was furious at the turn of event. He slammed his palm on the wall, "Damn! I cannot believe they easily carted away with my father's corpse."

His friend clasped him on the shoulder, "their potency was mightier,

Ovie, let it be. Let your father's soul find rest. You have troubled his body enough. I think we should go to the village and apologise."

Ovie brushed his hand aside, "Dave, you bother over little things. My father has not been buried, they dare not."

"Were you deaf when uncle Mamus said he witnessed the burial? Were you blind when he showed us pictures of the ceremony? Ovie get this straight, they have put your father in the ground and covered him with dust. It is over."

"No, it is not over. We shall exhume his body and bury him where he belongs."

"I think you've gone mad. It is so hot in here," Dave went to the bar and fixed himself a glass of juice with ice cubes.

"I am not. However, I will be. I will be mad if we do not do right by my father."

"Forget it Ovie, your father is resting in Godere, peacefully. We will go and apologise."

"We will get his body. Come on, Dave, we have to do this. You promised you got my back on this."

"Well, I have reached my final limits to that selfless oath I took. Count me out on this one," Dave sipped his drink.

"You can take the first flight back to the city," Ovie said. "I shall do it myself." Dave cocked an eyebrow.

Ovie's mother walked in, "you will do no such thing. Son, what is wrong with you. Was this how your father and I raised you? For goodness sake, what has come over you? Stop this madness please."

Ovie pointed at his mother, "You are a traitor for going over to Godere for his burial. Stay out of this, mother. You will not meddle in my affairs."

"This is my late husband you are raving about. I will not be silent and watch you disregard your father. Let him rest in peace. What is so special about burying him here? You will honour your father's request. His last wish was to rest in Godere despite your insistence."

"Everybody should stay clear of my decisions. I will not hesitate to crush anyone that comes in the way."

His mother stood close to him, their faces inches apart, "where were you when Godere youths were at their best, coward."

"Mother, you will not taunt me in that manner. Do not dare me."

Mamus walked in, "Ovie, do not talk to your mother that way," he said.

Her tone softened. "Calm down, my son. Your father was a traditionalist, and his clan has given him the burial rites that accorded his faith. You should apologise to your relatives. They shall grant you the honour of completing the final rites."

"That will be over my dead body. I shall bury my father the way I want."

"Ovie, you talk like an insane man," she thundered.

"Oh, just shut up, mother."

"Ovie, watch your utterances." His uncle gave him a slap, "she is my sister, your mother and your father's widow."

The force of the slap moved Ovie's face sideway. It took a while before Ovie turned his neck and faced his uncle. He flexed his shoulder. "Uncle, you slapped me?" he asked unbelievably.

"Yes, and believe me, I will slap you countless times if you say another disrespectful word to your mother. I have endured your nonsense for this long because you are my nephew, but no more. I thought your behaviour was born out of the frustration of losing your father. I looked upon you as a child with some tantrums, oh, Ovie; I forgot you are no more a child. I must look like a fool for supporting you all these while. I tried to convince you it is the way of your father's people to bury him according to custom." Ovie shook his head. He bowed to his mother and left the house.

Dave could not look at Ovie's mother. He went into the room and returned with his bag, "I am sorry, please forgive me ma. I will leave for the city at once." He left the house to take a commercial bus.

In the midnight, Ovie took some men to evacuate his father's coffin and buried it in Apele. Day and night, there was sorrowful cry of an adult man. This made the neighbours lost sleep. They requested Ovie and his family to come to their house and find out the mystery.

"I have played the oracle; it says your father's spirit is restless at where he was buried," said Mamus.

"I said it. I said my father should not be buried in the village." Ovie fervently said.

"Shut up. Your father's spirit is not restless in Godere. Someone removed his body from his grave. Ovie, your father's spirit desire to be back in his root, someone removed your father's body and put that of a dead stranger. His soul cries in Godere. He said whoever exhumed his body should bring it back to its rightful place."

Ovie's mother turned on him with suspicion, "Ovie, where have you kept his body?"

"I do not know, you should ask his relatives. Ask them if they took the body from the morgue and buried it in Godere or if they did something else with your husband's body."

His mother slapped him. "Ovie, tell us what you have done with your father's body?"

"I said I do not know. Do you people want to force a lie out of my mouth?" Ovie shouted.

A thunderous slap landed on Ovie's cheek. It was his mother that slapped him, "Tell me where my husband is you foolish child! If you don't tell me in a second, I will get naked and curse you here and now!"

Ovie quickly ran towards the hallway. His family followed him. Ovie had buried his father in one of the guest bedrooms.

"This is an abomination. Ovie, what have you done to your father?" Mamus calmly asked.

His mother covered her mouth in shock, "I was right. You are mad," she said.

"I just wanted to bury my father the way I want. This is his house, is it not? It is a tradition to also bury people in their houses?" Ovie slid to the floor and cried, "I have a right to bury my father the way I want."

Ovie's mother invited some youths to take the corpse back to Godere. Ovie paid some money as a levy for his act. The villagers pardoned Ovie and allowed him perform the final rites of the burial.

Four

The Danger of Self Medication

Iya tried to feed her son some herbal mixture. The child's flaying legs toppled the cup and the brown liquid content spilled on some coloured panties stacked on a low bench. Iya hissed at the mess. She imprisoned his tiny legs with her arm, and used the other to pin down his hands. She smiled at the workable tactics.

She poured another warm brew from the flask into the cup. Iya held her son's nose. Due to blockade of his nose, the baby breathed through his mouth. She poured the herbal brew into his tiny mouth and the medicine gurgle down his throat. His mother let go of him. He let out a cry and began kicking his leg in protest of the bitter taste.

Sissy came by the store, "it is wrong to give such a little baby agbo-herbal mixture to drink," she took the baby from his mother. She gently rubbed his back and fanned his face with her mouth. The baby stopped crying and hiccupped.

"It works well for sugar belly," Iya said. She stood up and separated the good pants from the stained pants, "how will I recover this loss?" She looked worn-out.

31

"That is your business, Iya, so figure a way out. I am angry with you. I just went to the slaughterhouse to get meat and you fed him agbo."

"I only wanted to cure his belly off sugar."

"Iya, you only gave him a wrap of chocolate to eat. Children actually need sugar for growth, it helps them become bright."

"That chocolate was too sweet. All the worms in his tummy will be dancing by now."

"That is why you should deworm your child in every three months," Sissy raised three fingers to Iya's face.

"Sissy, three months is too far. The agbo that I have given him will make my husband and I sleep well at night."

"Iya, this mixture is dangerous. The pharmaceuticals are not fools for making drugs that weaken and eliminate worms. Unknowing, you might be feeding him poison."

"Agbo worked for me, it will work for my child."

"It did work for you, yes. How well does it work for you? When last did you go to the hospital for check-up? Perhaps, in our days, the natural foods we fed on revitalized these strong herbs. You attended antenatal at the hospital, do not desist from their medical prescriptions for your baby. Agbo is not an approved medicine by NAFDAC or WHO. Most of these herbalists just brew all sorts of leaves and tree stems without accurate measurement and sell to people."

"My sister, agbo works at any time and on anybody. The midwives sanction agbo for ila-measles treatment. You know, and I know that it works well. Agbo is a component of powerful herbs."

"Yes, I know, but the substance you constantly give to your child, I have my doubts. Please stop giving my fine baby this stuff to drink. His system may not agree with it."

"But his system agrees with eating sweets? Hmmm, he will drink agbo to wash out the sweetness." The baby urinated on Sissy. "Oh, dear, I am sorry; he has ruined your dress."

"It is okay. Why did you not wear him diapers? Would you prefer to tie leaves around his waist?" Sissy rocked the baby and pecked his cheeks.

Iya laughed, "I will wear him pampers. If he eats another sweet, I will give him agbo to drink. A person that does not like bitter leaf should not be fond of eating sweets."

"Iya, I have warned you." Sissy sighed and handed the baby to his mother.

"So Sissy baby, which of the pants will you buy?" Iya spread many pants on the table, "your man will love this red colour very well. It matches your nail polish."

"I have not worn the pants I bought the last time jare. I have been too busy to go to my boyfriend's house for a weekend. I will only take two black bras. I need them for the white polo shirts I will wear for a two-day awareness walk. It is a campaign for people to stop self-medication. I will like you to attend. It is for people like you that like to administer drugs themselves, worse of all, traditional medicines."

"Who will look after my business while I roam the streets with placards and banners? Please, I am too hungry to get involved in your campaign, I cannot afford the walk, and I do not have the strength. I am looking for money. Sissy, maybe I will attend some other time."

"Iya, life is not all about making money. Iya, you should also learn how to use it. You can save up the Fifty Naira for agbo to buy worm medicine in the next three months. Please, you should pay attention to important programmes, especially those with health benefits. If you lock the shop for a day, there will not be loss in your business or profit margin. The kinds of goods you sell allow most of your customers to wait for you or come back again if you are not around. They can call you on phone when they are in urgent need of an item."

"Okay, I have heard you. I will join the campaign. Is it not just to walk about to share flyers and raise posters above my head?"

"It is not just that, you will take home lessons that are applicable to your health and practice it."

"Okay, thank you Sissy, I will see you tomorrow."

The next day, Iya was shelving her goods when Sissy came by. "Aha, Iya, you are displaying your goods. I told you the programme is by eleven o'clock, and this is past ten o'clock."

Iya adjusted her headgear. It loosened. She removed it and tied the scarf around her petite waist, "eh Sissy, the thing is. I cannot make it today. You see, today was market sanitation and it took an extra thirty minutes before the meeting ended. We opened the market just five minutes ago, so I want to make up for lost sales, I hope you understand."

"Iya…you should just lock the shop until we are back. I will help you arrange your wares and sell for the day."

"Sissy, please not today, I cannot make it. Please do not be annoyed. You know I am the only one fending for the family. My husband is yet to get another job. I am trying to raise capital for him to start a small business."

"Yes Iya, I understand. I wish I could help," Sissy's eyebrows furrowed.

"Sissy, your patronage is an assurance that we make profit and be able to keep body and soul together. Please tell more of your friends to patronize underclothes from me. I will sell at good prices," she started fixing the finest, sexy pants into hangers.

"Sure I will, Iya. I will be on my way. I will share useful information when I return. How is your son? You did not bring my fine boy to the shop?" Sissy peered into the shop.

"He stayed home with his father today. Let him babysit for today."

"That is good. Iya, I will see you later. Send my love to my fine boy," Sissy left and Iya fully opened her shop.

After she made some sales, Iya added up the money to previous sales and counted. She looked sad at the total sum spread in her palms. She rummaged through her wooden coffer and came up disappointed. Invoices, kola nut, old pen and some torn naira notes were all that filled the box.

"God, I am far from gathering substantial amount for my husband to start his phone repair business. God, please boost sales so I can raise enough money." Iya got up and propped up her goods to attract customers. She sang as she mopped her veranda.

Iya closed the shop very late. She reached home and flung her bag on the nearest chair. Her son was in a feverish condition, "Kenny, why did you not call me?" She bundled her son into her arms.

"I did not want to disturb you. He has had warm temperature since 4 pm, it worsened this night, like an hour ago," Kenny brought agbo to feed the boy.

Iya pushed the cup of agbo away. "No, he is not getting better. Do not give him the herb. Let us take him to the hospital," she said.

Kenny was frantic. He hurried into the bedroom and changed from his boxers to a trouser. They left for the hospital in anxiety.

The hospital admitted the child. "Madam, what have you been treating your child with? He is in a severe condition," the doctor said.

"Doctor, he has been well, he was not sick," Iya said in a weepy tone.

"He has been sick for a long time, the symptoms were not clear to you. He is very sick," the doctor scribbled on the baby's medical report card.

"Oh, my God, what sickness is that?" Kenny asked. He looked pale all of a sudden.

"What did you give him before coming here, what drugs have you given him?" The doctor asked.

"Agbo sir, it is usual to give him herbal medicine to cure his sugar belly because some nice patrons at my shop do give him sweet things to eat and drink." The doctor shook his head. Iya held the doctor's arms and went on her knees, "Doctor, please save my son. I cannot bear any other child. Please, his birth was complicated. My Doctor removed my womb to stop the infection from spreading. My son is my life."

"Madam, we are doing our best. We will run a test on him. Nurse, please get his blood sample."

"Please save our son," Kenny said.

"We will do our best. Nurse, get the blood test done with immediacy." The doctor patted Kenny's shoulder and left the room.

Some minutes later, the doctor said to the nurse, "nothing can be done for the child. He has few hours to live. The herbal components have cut his liver and opened holes in his kidney, whatever that was mixed in the substance was acidic. It was too toxic for a boy who has not clocked a year old."

The nurse looked at Iya and her husband, "oh, it is a pity. I wish a

37

miracle could happen. This horrible news will shatter the couple," she said.

"Doctor," Iya screamed. The doctor and nurse ran into the room. He put the thermometer on the boy's chest. He sighed. He gestured for the nurse to cover the corpse.

Iya stopped the nurse. She turned to the doctor, "Doctor, what is she doing?"

"I am sorry madam, we lost him," the doctor said.

Iya screamed and whipped her body on the floor. She grabbed the doctor's robe. "Do not take away my child from me. Look, I have money," she threw the sales money at the doctor, "take all the money and treat my child. Doctor, please bring my child back to life." She turned to the nurse, "I am sure you are a mother; you know I will not be able to live without my child. I cannot live through this pain."

Kenny dragged her into the hallway. She was kicking and crying, "Someone should bring back my child."

Kenny shook her roughly, "stop this Iya. Our precious son is no more. He is dead." Iya went quiet. Kenny laughed insanely. He dropped to the floor and cried.

Five

Mudlark

My brother and I sat in front of a local pharmacy. My feet hurt from walking about. My mother came out of the drugstore. "Mama, I am tired. I feel so weak. Can we not stay home today?" I said to my mother.

Mama swallowed some pills and drank water. She sat on a crate and massaged her hands and legs, "we must work hard, or else there will not be food for us to eat. Come on, we have to hurry to make some money. The pain will disappear once you walk around," Mama said as she tagged us along to the big market.

As much as I could remember, it had always been hard work all day if we must survive. Things only got worse after our eviction from Ileoda. The turbulent sea had threatened to submerge our community. The government marked down the waterfront and issued an eviction letter to residents of Ileoda.

The Minister of Housing and Environment had said it was for the good of its dwellers. The government said the reason was to build better houses for us. We tried to fight against it because these decent structures would not have a place for *low lives* like us. The restructuring roadmap of Ileoda did not include avenues for the poor. The government only wanted to get us out of the waterfront with no plans for settlement and they succeeded.

We were miserable and powerless to fight the government. Later, we were happy to get a court injunction, but the battle won, was short lived. The demolishers ignored the court injunction. They brought bulldozers to our homes and destroyed everything.

The demolition of houses and properties caused displacement of over fifty thousand residents of Ileoda. Many had nowhere to go. Some people expressed their displeasure by committing suicide. My family and I slept under different bridges for weeks until we were able to rent a room.

We reached the big market. My brother and I carried goods on our heads while Mama stacked customers' items on a plank sitting on her head and walked toward the motor park. As Mama was crossing the road, a speedy ambulance vehicle hit her. She died on the spot. We became orphans.

The caretaker threw out our merger belongings from the daily rented one room apartment, "go live in the slum. That is where you belong. Get out of here you scums of the earth."

The apartment was in the bowels of a slum. I wondered what other slum the caretaker meant. My brother and I became homeless. We moved to the shantytown where other children like us lived.

Some had run away from home. Others wandered off from the last spot their parents had asked them to wait and could not retrace their steps.

We slept by the sewer, on cartons and sacks. On cold nights, both of us slept in rusty drum. Our food came from dumpsites and alms. My brother died of cholera. Some boys and I wrapped him in a sack and threw him in the sea. They had told me to bury him on ground, but I did not want that. I did not need a close reminder of my brother's death.

To get rid of the pains, I tasted marijuana for the first time. I became an addict. At age fifteen, weed was a healing for me. It rimmed my eyes bloodshot. Every wrap I smoked, drowned my sorrow. I was glad I could forget those moments of pain. We ventured into street gang robbery.

I was smoking weed. The oldest of the gang handed a gun to me, "Ergo, you are still on your first wrap of weed; this means we will be late by the time you are on the sixth wrap. The boss is counting on us to deliver a good job," he banged my chest, "we cannot fail," he said.

"I know, I know. This assignment will prove the toughest we will embark on. After today, we will get our settlements from any robbery operation," I rubbed the gun, "this weapon is sophisticated; it will carry out an impressive job."

He took the gun from me, "you will get this when you are done."

I smoked the weed and trapped the smoke in my mouth. I exhaled through my nose and the fume cloud over my face.

Across the canal, I saw children bound off to school with their school bags and lunch packs. I went by the river. I was meditative for a while, trying to see a different future of me going to school. Going to school had been an expensive dream. We had attended a public school; the distance was miles and miles away.

Every day, we had walked on empty stomach. The day my brother fainted on the road, my mother stopped us from going to school. On that day she said, *'I will make money and send you to that school that is under the bridge, they pay Fifty Naira daily.'*

I called out my brother's name. I sought his soul to protect me as I embark on the mission. I saw something indefinable dart across the water. Suddenly, a vague human form appeared in front of me and entered my body very fast. I walked back to the settlement. I picked my most prized possessions in this world-my bracelet and family album. I did not tell the gang I was leaving. I took a stroll and left the slum.

A gang member met me on the road, "Ergo, where are you going?" he asked.

"My head is heavy. I am going for a short walk. I will be back before the operation. I want to play with my weapon."

"But we are yet to receive the weapons. The guns are still with the gang leader."

"Not that gun, my manly gun. I want to shoot some quick shots," I gave him a cocky grin. "You know what I mean?" I let him assume I was going to have sex. He thought I was going to the matured food seller, the woman that deflowered me in a dark alley when I newly came to the slum.

"Oh, I know. Take it easy, that your woman is oversized," he gave me a cocky grin and walked away.

Some hours later, I stood before the scene of the robbery I would have taken part. None of the gangs survived. Our boss laid an ambush; it was his plan to eliminate us. This would have been the last operation we did just for cocaine. We robbed for him and got cocaine in exchange for our services. He had agreed to pay us for every deal.

The spirit left my body. I saw my brother standing in front of me. *'I knew you would not listen to me if I had told you not to embark on the robbery. You would have joined the gang, despite my warning of danger,'* Fergo, my brother said.

He stepped aside and my mother appeared before me. She shook her head sorrowfully. She stretched her hands, I wanted to put my hand on her hand, but she withdrew. She held my brother's hand.

They stood together for a moment. I stared hard at them. My mother tapped her wrist. My brother smiled at me and they disappeared. I put on my bracelet, tears slid down my cheeks.

I did not return to the slum. I slept at a fuel station. In the morning, I begged the car wash operators to allow me join the business. After much hesitation, they agreed to give me a trial. They gave me a branded t-shirt. I was grateful for the opportunity and nice shirt.

I washed ten cars that day and got a plate of rice and water for my hard work. I was satisfied. I slept in the mechanic workshop; it was cosier than the slum.

One day, a customer forgot his wallet on the seat. I ran after him and called out, "excuse me Oga, you left your wallet on the chair."

He collected the wallet and brought out One Thousand Naira note. He shouted, "My money is missing." His alarm attracted a crowd.

"Oga, that was how I found your wallet," I said.

"Shut your mouth, stupid thief. Bring back my money, or else I will deal with you," he raised his hand to slap me.

"Oga, I am saying the truth. The moment you stood up from the seat, I rushed after you with the purse. I swear I did not take your money," I touched a finger to my tongue.

"You do not want to say the truth, right? I see you are an expert in stealing," he brought out his phone and dialled a number.

"Please sir; I do not know anything about the missing money. I swear by my dead mother." People gathered around the fuel station, suspicious eyes were on me.

"Bring a tube and fuel, we will teach him a lesson," a man said. In an instant, someone covered my head with a bucket.

"Are you a fool? Do you want to burn down the fuel station?" The Manager shouted and asked the security man to ward off the mob.

The car wash boys pounced on me. They beat me up with mop sticks and hose. "Please sir, I swear I was a thief but I have changed. I did not take your money." I screamed as the beating increased.

"That is enough. Please let him go. I will not come here to wash cars again." The man entered his car and drove off. They beat me some more, stripped me to my pant and threw me out of the fuel station.

I strolled down the road, unaware of my nakedness. A mad man threw a stone at me. He gestured for me to come over and sit by him. I shook my head. He stood up angrily and charged at me. I ran away as fast as I could. I found a tattered wrapper in a dumpsite. I tied it around my waist, and used the upper edges to crisscross my neck.

I strolled until I came to an old motor garage. I saw a food vendor and salivated over the aroma from the meals. I walked to the woman. "Madam, mother, please give me food," I opened my palms in a beggarly manner.

She scornfully appraised me. "Are you crazy? Do I look like your mother? Leave my shop before I insert this spoon in your eyes." The spoon came dangerously close to my eyes. I shifted back. In an instant, she poured water on me from a bowl. It smelled like soup, I licked it off my hand.

"Haba madam Mealy, why are you harsh on the poor boy? How much is my bill? Please, give him food from the change you owe me," a kind customer said. I smiled at him.

"I will not sell food to this smelly thing. I cannot let him put infested hands on my plate."

"Madam Mealy, you have disposable plates, please give him food. The boy is very hungry."

"No, he should leave my shop, please. You can collect your change, he should buy food elsewhere." She hissed and went back to selling food.

The man stood. He was angry. He said to madam Mealy, "your food tastes like poison in my mouth. I will not come here to eat any more." Other customers stopped eating. They stood up to leave the shop.

"Madam Mealy, your attitude is bad. What kind of a woman are you? Do you not have children? We are very angry at your bad actions today," another customer said.

Madam Mealy knelt, "please my customers stay and finish your meal. I will give the fine boy food. The bill is on me. Fine boy come and take food." She served a bowl of rice with assorted meat. She called a salesgirl to bring soft drink and water.

I knelt. I generously thanked the kind customers and Madam Mealy. I sat on the floor to eat. When I finished eating, I packed other customers' plates to the back of the shop. I washed the plates.

The salesgirl was instructing me on where to put the plates when Madam Mealy said softly, "will you take your dirty self out of my sight? You want to bring bad luck to my business," she pushed me away. I dropped the plates on the table and wanted to walk through the door. She stopped me. She held my ear and dragged me to a narrow passage, "follow that small gate, and you will find yourself at the main road."

As soon as I came out, I saw the fuel station I had washed cars. I became frightened. The man I returned his wallet beckoned me. I went to him, "I came back to look for you. I found my money, I am sorry."

He took me to an eatery, "My name is Godwin," he said.

"I am Ergo," I smiled. He bought some pastries-meat pie and a pack of juice for me. He asked about my family and I told him everything. The man took me to his house. All his kids were grown. I found a wonderful family-parents, and siblings. For their family vacation, they took me to America.

Six

Read and Lead

T here was a flurry of activities in the office. The Manager came to the Secretary's desk, "the keynote speaker just called. She will be late for the book reading. We will have to put her name as the last speaker."

"But the pamphlets have already been printed," the Secretary said.

"The copies are detachable and with the Printer. The Printer will only insert a page. Debo, you know what to do, do not make me exert my energy. We have a big day tomorrow. Edit the name of the speakers and forward to the Printer, it must be ready by tonight. Afterwards, take the pamphlets to the venue. Check if all the arrangements are good to go. Once confirmed, transfer the next instalment to the event planner."

"Yes sir," Debo settled in his desk. He typed and sent the e-mail. Afterwards, he called the speaker's Personal Assistant.

"Babe, how are doing?" He listened and nodded at her responses, "I am fine, doing great. If I may ask, what is wrong with the convener of Fly Girl Foundation?" he listened attentively, and then tilted his lip, "she is down with menstrual cramps. Clara, is it because of some red bloodstains my boss has to put me under pressure? Sometimes, I wonder what women are doing in the corporate world. If the cramp is going to make her late, it is possible she will not show up at the event. You women can do the world a favour if you just stay at home and nurse your womanly issues." His girlfriend argued on the other end, her voice was not perceptible, "your boss is your role model right? Look here babe; we should be clear on this. A week to our marriage, you are going to quit your job. I do not want my wife to work. You will stay at home and take care of our family."

Her tone was loud now, "that will not happen. You met me as an executive and that is what I will remain. After all, my kind of job avails me time to take care of personal matters."

"I see, listen babe. If we were getting married, you would have to quit your job. You choose either your job or me. The choice is yours."

"Come on, babe, why are you this insensitive? We will talk it over at dinner next tomorrow." Debo was silent. He wore an irritated look. "Hello dear…Did you hear me? We will talk things over. You and my job are important to me. I will see you at dinner, right?" Debo vexingly hung the call. He went to the press and waited for the pamphlets to be printed. At completion, he took the event programs to the event hall.

Clara stared at her employer who was wreathing on the couch. Debo's call challenged her to do something about her boss's predicament. She decided to make her boss feel better. She searched her handbag for medicine. "Madam, have these pills. It will kill the pains fast."

Angelica overlooked the drugs, "sorry Clara, I am stressing you. You should be asleep. Tomorrow is a big day for us."

"I am fine, madam. Let us get this pain to pass or else there may not be a big day. You look pale and weak."

Angelica shook her head at the pills, "I am not a lover of pills. Besides, I do not take drugs for these periods. The menstrual cycle is a natural course for a woman. For me, I like to bear the pain. I do not want to be reliant on drug."

"Madam, you are yet to read your speech. That is because you have been wincing."

"I trust you did a great job. I need an early rest. By tomorrow, I will be strong. The only problem I have is my heavy flow. My sanitary towel is not absorbing it. I stuck cotton wool in my vagina before I wore the pad. It makes me feel uneasy. The flow is unusual. I wonder how I am going to manage tomorrow."

"And you have to be comfortable for tomorrow's event. Madam, I think you should just have the painkillers," Angelica shook her head, "okay, and do not worry, madam. I have the right towel for you. It will keep you dry and fresh." Clara brought out a pack of sanitary towel from her shower bag.

"Is this Nigerian made?"

"Yes madam, this is made in Nigeria."

"No, no, this will cause a mess. I do not trust Nigerian products."

“Please, madam, just try it out. Please,” Clara said persuasively.

“Okay I will. Please bring me a plate of pepper soup. I will be in my bedroom. I will shower again and try this on.” She waved the pad in the air.

Clara broke the painkillers into the soup and stirred for some minutes. She prayed her boss did not notice.

* * * * * *

In the morning, Angelica came downstairs refreshed and dressed for the occasion, “Clara good morning,” she smiled warmly.

“Good morning, madam, you look radiant. Here is a list of today’s activities.”

“Thank you, Clara,” she accepted the note, “we will make it early to the book reading. Thank you for the sanitary towel. I woke up dry; it adsorbed the heavy flow so well. It feels the sanitary towel has a healing effect. The cramps are gone. I usually feel relieved after forty-eight hours. That worked like magic. Please order that sanitary towel, I need a room full,” she twirled around the room. She read the paper presentation and nodded satisfactorily, “great job, you write my thoughts and belief in a passionate way that I feel you live in me. Well done, Clara.” She gave back the paper to Clara.

Clara collected the paper and clipped it to a file. “Thank you, madam.”

They were punctual at the event. Some delegates were signing into the hall. Clara registered the boss's name and they proceeded to admire the décor arrangements of the event.

Debo was shocked to see them. Angelica went around exchanging pleasantries with other speakers and some familiar delegates she knew. Debo and Clara spoke in low tones. She told him how she gave her boss a painkiller.

The event progressed. It was time for Angelica's speech. After the introduction of her topic, she cast the paper aside and spoke from the heart, "as humans we tend to stride on sustainable growth, it is a natural feeling for any right thinking individual. We should deal in what we can handle and be consistent in it.

Do not take on what you cannot lift onto your shoulder and take off your shoulder except you have helping hands to accomplish heavy tasks with you. To all readers gathered here, we should picture ourselves as leaders, leaders that are unstoppable, let no pain hold you down, let no weight weigh you down, and you must reach for that height.

To reach your goal, you must cultivate a habit that consistently grows and not diminishes you. Reading enhances greatness, those who read, seek wisdom, the reader becomes wise, the reader becomes a principal. Read a book today, you will relearn vastness."

The audience applauded excitedly. Debo clapped admiringly and stared at Clara. She smiled at his enthusiasm and gave a thumb up to Angelica.

Seven

The City That Never Sleeps

I woke up and checked the wall clock; the time was 2:45 in the morning. I jumped out of bed and grabbed my phone. The phone was off. That was why my alarm failed to wake me up by 2 am. The annoying tone can disrupt one's deep slumber and its insistent shrieking loudness can wake up the dead.

I walked to the bathroom like a sleepwalker. I brushed my teeth while I turned on the shower. I reached for my towel but the rail was empty. The previous evening, I hung my towel outside and forgot to bring it in. I was in a hurry.

I dried my body with my white singlet. I did not have time to get my towel. I wore the wet singlet; it will not be noticeable in my company's black polo shirt. I put on my underwear, trouser, and shoe. I sprayed many perfume on my cloth and perceived the refreshing fragrance. That will do! I grabbed my shirt and office bag.

I did not wear my shirt-a small trick by any man that had to leave the neighbourhood before dawn. At this hour, some persons tend to be maniacs on the street. I left the house at exactly three o'clock. I will make it to the bus stop in the next five minutes. I patted my pocket to make sure the small knife was intact.

I always put a dagger in my pocket. Heading out at this time could be unsafe. Any passer-by might turn out to be a pickpocket if they see a well-dressed person, so I look unpredictable without a shirt on. The likely culprits were bound to keep out of my way.

I saw two dark figures coming towards me. I slid my hand into the pocket and held my knife tightly. My hand relaxed on the weapon when they passed me. I breathed heavily until I reached the bus stop. It was flooded with passengers and there were fewer buses.

I needed to get moving. I must reach the designated point the company bus was parked. My workplace was so far from my residence. I filled Ikeja as my residential address because the advertisement specified the applicants must live within Ikeja, Berger or Ikorodu area of Lagos State.

I lived at Alakija. I applied for the job because it was the ideal job for me. I lied I live in Ikeja. Therefore, when the company bus dropped me at Ikeja bus stop, I usually found my way home from there. The transportation cost took most of my salary. I did not mind because the job experience I was gaining was more than the pay. When I start my own business, these experiences will fetch me reliable profits.

I got on a bus. The city was busy. Hoarders had begun to market their goods. I bought a shaving stick to trim my beard. The moment I had a less busy weekend, I would visit the barber for a proper cut. I looked at the rear-view mirror and the image of a mad man stared at me.

I grinned and got ready to alight from the bus.

I sighted the company's bus and hurried as the backlight beamed to move. I powered on my phone. The one per cent battery level was enough to make a call. I called the driver, "hello Captain Dele, please hold on for me." I got on the bus panting. I greeted my senior and junior colleagues. The AC dried my sweat and I relaxed into the posh chair.

I had a fulfilled day at work. I got a promotion. I became the Head of Digital Operations and the company gave me an official car. I wanted to drive the car home despite knowing I might encounter bad traffic. Ikeja municipal was usually a congested area with unmoving vehicles. I stopped by the ATM to withdraw cash. I will need it for tonight's groove with some friends.

At the foot of Dopemu Bridge, I encountered a terrible hold up. It took three hours to ascend and descend the short bridge. A bus driver told me a trailer fell and blocked the road. It would not be possible to get home in this situation. I veered into a fuel station and parked my car. I gave the security man some money to help me guard the car until I come for it tomorrow morning.

I would have taken a bike but motorcycles did not ply the major road. The boardwalk was crowded. I stepped down to the road for a while, but climbed onto the boardwalk because it was dangerous. I joined many others to walk as slow as a snail.

The gridlock ended at Isheri round about. Many commuters were at the bus stop because buses were behind in traffic. My feet were sour from walking, and I could not take more steps.

An exotic car stopped in front of me, I shifted away from it. The driver beckoned, I did not bulge, "are you going to Lasu road? I can give you a lift. I am off to Ojo," the strange driver said.

I was alarmed that a fellow man wanted to give me a ride. I walked towards the car but stopped when he asked other stranded people to stay away. I became suspicious of the driver and backed out. He drove away without looking back. I tore the side of my trouser and transferred my cash into my tight underwear-it gave my crotch a bulge. I have heard that some crooks could use voodoo to tell if a person had money on him.

I failed to get into three buses. On the fourth trial, I attempted to get on a slow moving bus. I was tumbling when someone grabbed my hand from within and pulled in my upper body. I suspended my body in that position until other people backed out when they realised only a seat was vacant. I got in and thanked my helper.

It was midnight. I dropped at Iyana Iba. The locale was crowded with people and vehicles. Lagos was a busy state. This city did not slumber because it was the central point of Nigeria's industrialisation. All kinds of business flourished in Lagos metropolis and pastoral districts. In this city, many individuals visualised and accomplished their dreams. The opportunities that abound in this state were vast.

This was why I applied for a job far away from my residential area. To strike it big, I had to move out of my comfort zone. The struggle to be successful and survive in this city was tough. It was worthwhile when one got-a good job, house, sufficient account balance to sustain the family needs and any luxury money could buy.

Most residents of Lagos were busy from dawn to dark. While some people were laying their beds to go to sleep, other people were coming out to do business. I bought bread. I stylishly deepened my hand into my pant to get the money, but it was gone. Someone had robbed me in my haste to get onto the bus.

I smiled and dropped the bread. I apologized to the saleswoman and walked away. I had no money on me. I trekked and got home by 1 am. I had an hour to sleep before I would wake up and prepare for work. There was hardly time for me to rest and have a good night sleep. I fell on the bed with my clothe on and slept.

Eight

A Taste of Racism

My job was to shine hundred pots in a day. A jarring task I had to do for eighteen hours a day. I whistled in excitement as I polished a big pot. My hands looked rough like that of a tortured slave. I put my hands on the working table.

Under the florescent, it looked like a map of misery. I was not perturbed with my status, I had pictures of my forbearers been slaves. My great-grandfather was lucky to trace his root back to the Western Delta in Nigeria.

I got my notepad and continued the development of my short story. The story was due for submission to an online journal. I prayed the Journal accept my submission. I had gotten several rejections in the last six months. I was on the last paragraph when a bell squawked across the factory. It was lunchtime. I left my phone to charge in the Changing Room. I went to the cafeteria, brooding over the menu as usual.

The Management had added African foods to the menu timetable. However, it was yet to get an African cook. The Chef put some foods in my plate. He sniffed the aroma and smiled with satisfaction. I took the plate and sneered at the boiled turkey with salad, and a cup of fresh carrot juice. I thought most Africans' habit of eating heavy foods was associated with gaining strength and not an eating disorder.

I usually felt like a bird after eating these light meals. It did not energize me for the heavy task I had to accomplish. Carbohydrates had strong nutrient, which strengthened black people to do hard labour.

If my ancestors had depended on vegetables, they would have been frail hopeless slaves, whipped to death because they could not do hard labour. Hard bread, many starchy foods were the food of strength for slaves. Their masters knew this too well.

My colleague, Fox, gave me an awry look, "Onos, you are not eating your meal," he said.

Under his snooping stare, I began to pick at the vegetables. I ate some and dropped the cutleries. I could not pretend I relish the meal.

There was a restaurant called Calabar Kitchen, it was two blocks away. I needed to get to the African restaurant for my normal work diet. My Nigerian colleague had introduced me to the sumptuous vegetable soup with foo-foo-cassava flour. The meal had become my energizer.

"Fox, please hold up for me while I get something to eat. I will just be few blocks away."

"Okay, what about your meal? You are just going to waste good food. You will let it go to waste?"

"No, you can have it." Fox added the meal to his plate before I even took a step. I shook my head and walked away. I envied him because his job was to distribute the polish. The vegetable soup was prepared with dried fish and snail. I ate and was satisfied.

I returned to the factory and saw my messenger's red light beeping. I had a message from a friend. He was the one who introduced me to this journal I was writing to and he assured me my story was getting in its Fall Issue. I read the message wide eyed, '*Hey, I am deleting anyone with Nigerian contacts. Someone hacked my page some minutes ago. Are you sharing information with scammers? I am hooked up with American law enforcement officers to get rid of them...please respond to my request. Are you a Nigerian?*'

I read the message in confusion. This was coming from a new friend, Greg. I thought over my response. From his message, I deduced my nationality would offend him for some reasons. I wondered if he had something against Nigerians. How do I handle this situation? He was one of the few nice people I have met on social media. He was American. He had been teaching me cool ways on how to write a story.

He started *typing... 'Hey, I know you are there. You are reading my messages. All the Nigerians to Mr are swindle artists, are you one?'* This time he asked using a smiling emoticon. I wondered who this 'Mr' was. My phone beeped again; there was another message from Greg. '*Sorry, I meant *me* 'Mr' was a typo.*'

I asked him how he was. I told him I could not be a fraud. '*I am a responsible man.*'

'*Listen to me, my friend.*'

'*My name is Onos.*'

'*Whatever…We are having major issues. My phone has been hacked and all sorts of crap are being done with my user accounts. Therefore, I want to know if you are a Nigerian.*'

I was afraid of losing my new American friend. He seemed to be very angry with Nigerians. I pondered on what these crooks posing as white people and Nigerian Princes had done.

I typed, '*Oh, sorry about that Greg, it happens. Some bad people can hack anybody's account. The hacker can be from any race, unscrupulous nature is not peculiar to a nation. Greg, you just have to tighten your privacy and security settings. Also, do not open every link sent to your phone.*'

'*I am not mistaken. This is not about racial discrimination. I just received classified report that the hackers are from Nigeria. Are you a Nigerian?*'

I was a bit relieved to read this. I typed, '*really, they have traced the hacker to Nigeria?*' I sent a happy emoticon.

'*Yeah really, the silly hackers have been caught.*'

'*That is great. It is good you fished them out. That was a nice job. Well done.*'

'*So tell me, are you a Nigerian?*'

At this point, I knew my friendship with this American would wane. For a moment, I wanted to deny my nationality to save my friendship. '*Greg, I am a decent African. I am not a con artist. The first day we connected, you told me you sought my friendship because I am a creative. You were impressed with my short story I had posted on a platform, you found my page, and we became friends.'* I sighed deeply, hoping that would convince him.

'I know Mr, but the question is, are you a Nigerian?'

I braced myself for the consequences of my revelation, *'yes, I am a Nigerian. A full-fledged Nigerian, I was born and bred in Nigeria. I am here in America to work and find other respectable opportunities.'*

'That means you are a Nigerian.'

'Did you not read me? Maybe you should get your eyes checked. Yes, I am a Nigerian, a proud African-Nigerian.' I coughed and rushed to get water.

I returned to my laptop. Greg's message read, *'I cannot be friends with a con artist. It does not matter if you are not one of them. There should not be connectivity between us. Your friendship with me makes me vulnerable to swindlers, I have seen them cheat good people and I do not want to fall a victim. I am unfriending you right away.'*

Few minutes later, there was a notification from my facebook application. I had commented on his birthday post. His reply to my comment was, *'Thanks for the sentiments, Nigerian...I value real friendship.'*

Greg blocked me from accessing his facebook page. I was glad I owned up to my identity. He was not a worthy friend. It was funny his profile read, 'when the power of love is greater than the love of power...the world will know peace.'

Nine

A Test of Faith

A woman was in labour. Some people on the street could hear her screams. Those who could empathise with the excruciating pains she must be feeling took some moment to say a little prayer for the patient while others spared glances at the hospital.

After hours of prodding labour, the nurses and doctor delivered the woman of a baby boy. The baby was very big. The woman had a big tear in her vagina. She bled irrepressibly. She fainted several times and the doctor reinstated her with shocks. She was losing lot of blood. She was a believer that blood transfusion was not of God. Her husband prayed for God's intervention.

"Mr Jason, you need to agree to this transfusion in order to save your better half. You do not want your first child and this new born to be without their mother," Doctor Greg said.

Mr Jason pondered for some minutes. "No, I do not want to lose my wife. I cannot bear it. Please give her a blood transfusion," he said.

Mrs Jason was adamant, "Jason, why are you of little faith? I don't want a blood transfusion."

Mr Jason clasped her hands, "What should I do? I am so scared."

A nurse shouted, "Her blood pressure is dropping, we are losing her." Another nurse rolled the shocker machine to the bedside.

"Clear!" doctor Greg shocked her several times, "she is out of danger, for now. Her condition is stable for now; it will not be for long. She may not live beyond six hours. Mr Jason, you have to come to a decision. Your wife needs an urgent blood transfusion." Mr Jason was indecisive, "we can give the blood and you make payments later, I will stand as a surety." Doctor Greg said.

"It is not about the money. I can afford to buy the whole blood in that bank. This is about our faith. Our doctrines forbid blood transfusion," Mr Jason said.

"Mr Jason, this is about life and death. Religion is for the living. Only the living can covet faith, only the living can praise God. Remember, even God gave his beloved son's blood for us to live. Jesus Christ spilled his precious blood for us all to be clean and have everlasting life," Doctor Greg said.

"Doctor, this is different," Mr Jason said.

"Mr Jason, you talk of the Bible, why do you not live and act by the Bible. When it was necessary, Christ spilled his blood to save multitudes of people. The blood of Jesus saved uncountable souls. Look, do not be too hard on yourself. You can stand on your decision to give her some blood; we need to act on our sentiments at times like this. Mr Jason, please be religiously selfish for today. I understand your faith, but I do not encourage blind faith, for man has formulated these religious doctrines. Some rules were born out of personal conviction; it must not be adhered by a legion. Some rules can be broken. With your permission, we can sedate her. The sedation will last for a while; she would not know if any blood transfusion occurred, our hospital would keep it a top secret." Mr Jason had not been listening. Doctor Greg touched the absentminded man, "I hope you heard all I said?"

"I did doctor; please help me keep my wife safe. She has to be alive to take care of our children and me."

"I take that to be a yes?" The Doctor asked. Mr Jason nodded, "that is a good decision, cast all doubts aside. We will be fast with the transfusion."

Mr Jason's wife held his hands. She shook her head solemnly. Moist gathered in his eyes, her tears rolled down freely. Seeing this, Doctor Greg was shocked. He was speechless for a while. He had not seen a faith so strong. Mr Jason sat by his wife still holding her hands. He touched her hand to his forehead.

"Mr Jason, I am sorry I tried to talk you out of what you strongly believe in. Mrs Jason, if you can hear me, I am sorry I disregarded your faith. I just cannot see you die like this. My mother died while giving birth to me. I know what it feels like to grow up without a mother. I only pressured for this blood transfusion so that your children's fate would not be the same as mine. Believe me; if you die, the void you will leave in their hearts may not fill up with ease. Once again, please forgive me," doctor Greg said. He dabbed a tear and left the room.

He stood in the hallway for a long time and took a deep breath. He could hear Mr Jason crying. He sobbed too, thinking how someone could just stay helpless and do nothing to save a loved one. Doctor Greg could defy orders to save a life, but he was helpless in this case of faith and fate. He climbed down the stairs and overhead a conversation from one of the wards.

A mother was spoon-feeding her daughter pumpkin juice. She cajoled the young woman who found the greenish juice tasteless. "Drink it up, it will give you blood. This is the best blood substitute we can get for now," the woman said. Her daughter made sign of vomiting. She rubbed her back to soothe her.

After hearing this, Doctor Greg took the stairs two at a time. He rushed back to Mrs Jason's room. Mr Jason had fallen asleep on his wife's bosom. He stirred him, "does your religion forbid pumpkin leaves?"

"No, not at all," Mr Jason stood and mildly scratched his eyes.

"Then we can give her some as supplement."

"Yes, My God. What was I thinking? This skipped my mind. We can give her for blood supplement."

Mr Jason ran out of the room. There was a market close to the hospital. He hurriedly purchased every pumpkin leave available in the market. Out of excitement, he paid more than the stipulated amount.

Some nurses helped wash the leaves thoroughly and blended. They fed the broth to Mrs Jason. After a while, Mr Jason was overjoyed to see his wife recovering. Her breath became even and colour returned to her skin.

Mr Jason held Doctor Greg's hands, "thank you so much. God used you as an angel of life. We were too distraught to remember pumpkin leave as a supplement for blood. Some other doctor would have left us to our stringent faith."

"Love would not let me. Love is the greatest religion," Doctor Greg said. Mr Jason hugged him.

A nurse brought the newborn baby, "he has been crying. He refused to feed from the nursing mothers," she said.

"Give him to his mother. She is strong enough to feed him," Doctor Greg said. The nurse cooed the baby and handed him to Mrs Jason.

"Thank you, my milk is flowing. On my deathbed I heard his cries," Mrs Jason said. She kissed her baby and fed him.

"You are indeed a strong woman, God bless you all," Doctor Greg said.

"Thank you Doctor, God bless you too," Mr and Mrs Jason, said.

"I will be in my office, if you need anything, just press the intercom and I will come running to your room." They laughed and Doctor Greg left the room.

Ten

The Citizen Journalist

Sunripe Newspaper was a leading space for journalism. The firm was highly funded. It had an impressive number of staffs. Therefore, continual production and reproduction was definite. The challenging atmosphere made it a battleground as reporters set to deliver special breaking news across beats.

The photographers and camera operators returned with their visuals from covering an event. They had to put the newsworthy item together and serve hot to the audience. They got busy in the editing suite, reviewing contents. The reportage was an exclusive. Kola was the photographic editor. He had gotten tip-offs from some contacts and press releases to add more spice to the news.

They went through some archival material to search for an old footage in relation to the recent event. Kola filtered the noise and smiled at the polished overall work. As instructed by the copy-editor, he made effort to reach the Chief Editor. He succeeded in getting the Chief Editor's approval to put the news to bed.

In a meeting with some tennis club members, the Chief Editor halted his speech when he saw the viral video on television. He excused himself. He made a dash drive to the office. He did not pay attention to staffs' greetings. "Where is Kola?" He asked the Secretary.

"He is in the Newsroom," the Secretary said. She was jumpy.

"Tell him to come to my office." The Secretary scampered to the Newsroom. The Chief Editor briskly walked into his office and sat. He was furious.

Kola walked in, "good day sir, you sent for me."

"Yes Kola, take a seat. I will join you shortly," Kola sat. He felt uneasy with the way his boss looked at him from across his desk. The Chief Editor glanced through some paper reports and grunted. He brought a chair to sit in front of Kola. He stared long at him and cleared his throat.

"Kola, how long have you been working in this establishment?"

"It is one year and six months."

"And is that not enough time for you to accustom yourself to the duties of this prestigious firm?"

"Sir, I carry out assignments according to the rules and regulation of this honourable profession."

"I do not mean the general statements." He stood to the circled world map and turned it until it reached the African continent. He pointed at Nigeria, "this is Nigeria. Kola, here you do not report information with such level of honesty. That was very wrong of you, Kola, this is

Nigeria."

"But sir, what have I done wrong?"

"You have done everything wrong from covering the event of the tribal clash and to publishing it on our news website. It went viral; other media outfits have lifted the news and quoted us as source."

"It is our copyright, sir. They should give credit to Sunripe Newspaper."

"Kola, you still do not get it."

"I don't. Please, tell me what you are talking about, sir."

"The genocide was carried out in Gibbon. That is the home of our Publisher and her husband happen to be the Governor of that State. Now, the Publisher is angry with us all. Our jobs are on the line. For that damning report, you have put our credible source of livelihood on the line. I am at risk of losing my job, and it is all because of you. Your caption was such a grave sensation. Your conclusion of the story was that the State Government has a link to the genocide. 'The Government conducted a mass burial to hide its dirty linen.' That was our speculative conclusion, right?"

"Yes, sir."

"Kola, that was unimpressive."

"But sir, reliable sources gave that information. We reported the fact and as we speak, more details are trickling in. Further investigation shows the number of causalities and deceases are over four thousand. I will give more updates on the event as soon as possible."

"You will do no such thing. In fact, I want you to take down that post. On no account should news related issues on it be published by us. You will resign from this assignment."

"Sir," Kola raised his hand to make a point.

"You will not question my orders. You will do as I say."

"But sir, we cannot downplay the chaos going on in Gibbon. With your permission, I wish to take a team of reporters to the scene for follow up investigation."

"Did you lose my insinuation when I said the report on the website should not appear in print? Young man, we have nothing to do with the news reportage of this event."

"That would be violating the rules of journalism. It is our responsibility to tell the people what is happening around them. We are socially responsible to gather information on this heart-breaking incident in order to get possible aids and interventions from local and international agencies. As we speak, the victims have not received relieve materials and condolence messages from the Government and public sympathies."

"You know this job too well; indeed you studied your textbooks diligently. Nevertheless, this is practical. It is quite different from profound theories. For your stupidity, we are on the verge of losing our jobs. You will follow my instructions or lose your job."

Kola stood, "I will not keep my job at the detriment of human lives. Sir, with or without this company identification, I am still a Journalist. I can carry out my duties without Sunripe Newspaper. I am a trained journalist."

"You will roast in penury."

"I am not a brownnoser, brown envelops does not make me, I am a responsible Journalist. Hunger cannot kill my soul; it can only weaken my body. I want to do the right thing with free conscience and to bring honour to my profession. This is beyond money. Truth and justice are the greatest nourishments I need in my life."

"I see you are trying to play the hero," the Chief Editor sneered.

"I am just human, sir." Kola nodded and left the office.

As Kola walked down to the bus stop, he was resolute on his decision. He felt he made the best decision to quit his job with Sunripe Newspaper. He transferred more of the genocide pictures to his email and kept the phone in his laptop bag. A rowdy crowd drew his attention. Kola was in a hurry to catch a bus. He checked his wristwatch, "I can spare some minutes to see what the raucous is about." He said.

A frightened woman was about to be raped. Four men held her thighs, hands, and legs. A dirty looking man was pulling his pants to get on her. Kola dragged him off her and furiously punched him in the face.

The other men released her and went for Kola. He fought them off. He turned to the crowd, "You all are no better than those heathens. You take pictures and make video instead of coming to her aid. Your act is animalistic." Kola spat on the ground in disgust.

"She is a thief. We will treat her worse than an animal," someone

THE INVALID CITIZEN AND OTHER STORIES

from the crowd said.

Kola shoved the people that clustered around the victim and picked her up. "Are you okay?" Kola asked.

She nodded hysterically, "I did not steal anything. On entering the market," she pointed at the man that wanted to rape her, "that stinky tout harassed me. I slapped him and in turn, he threatened to deal with me. I did not take his words serious because I will not chance on him again, as I will not visit this market ever again. I was surprised when he raised an alarm of '*thief*'. He had pointed at me and started running towards my direction. Before I knew what was happening, an angry mob gathered. They tore my clothes and that beast was set to rape me," she broke down in tears and hugged her pieces clothes to her body.

The Police siren made the crowd scram. Kola was quick to rake the acclaimed rapist to the ground. He held the cynic by his shirt and thrust him to the Police, "Officers, that is the criminal, he tried to rape a woman." Kola said.

A Police Inspector handcuffed the suspect and put him at the back seat of the vehicle. The Inspector turned to the woman, "you will have to come with us to the station to give your statement."

The woman looked at Kola and he gestured for her to go with the Police. "I will accompany you," Kola said and smiled reassuringly. She nodded and entered the back seat of another vehicle.

Kola wanted to go in after her but the Inspector stopped him, "there is no space in this vehicle, do you mind taking the other," he pointed at an unbranded Hilux. I hope you do not have a problem with that?"

The woman looked apprehensive, "sure, no problem," Kola said and went over to sit in the Hilux. She smiled and relaxed somewhat.

Close to the police station, someone put a handkerchief to Kola's nose and he passed out. He regained consciousness and found himself in a dark room. He tried to free his hands from the tight rope, but the process tore his flesh.

"Who did this? Show yourselves you cowards!" Kola's voice echoed and phased out. The light header came fully on him.

"Within these walls of danger, he is still brave," a dark figure said.

"Show yourself you coward." Kola shouted.

"As you wish," the dark figure appeared to be the Chief Editor.

"You?" Kola was stunned.

"Yes, me. Your former boss…"

"So, it was you who got me kidnapped?"

"Yes, that's right, Kola. I was not comfortable after you left the office. The Police were the only people to take you out of the area without drawing suspicious stares. I just need to have a small talk with you."

"That woman, is she with you? Was she a bait to get me?" Kola looked furiously at the floor and clenched his teeth in anger. "She will pay for this."

"No, Kola, calm down, do not be too quick to judge the innocent woman. She was not part of the plan. I am glad her predicament delayed you. It gave the Police ample time to get to you. Listen well; the Governor said you have the video where he was paying off some

74

terrorists," he held Kola by the neck and choked him a little. "You can join the woman at the Police Station. That is if you cooperate with us." The Chief Editor signaled at some men who assembled some torturing equipment in front of Kola.

"What is it you want?" Kola asked.

"Where is the rest of the information? I want the whole detail."

"They are already in your possession," Kola said.

The Chief Editor told one of the thugs to get Kola's laptop bag. "Good boy, I always appreciate your mobile office sense."

The Chief Editor opened the bag and instructed Kola to delete every file in his email. Kola wiped off all the files and the Chief Editor formatted his laptop. Tears rolled down Kola's eyes because he had lost hundreds of personal projects in his computer storage.

"The lion is broken. I am glad we could handle this wild cat. I did not think it would be this easy," the Chief Editor looked at the goons and asked, "right boys?" They nodded and laughed sinisterly. Kola was broken. At night, they blindfolded Kola. They dumped him in the middle of the road.

The Chief Editor lustfully stared at his Personal Assistant. "Jane why were you not at my house this weekend?" He asked.

"Nothing sir," said Jane. She continued to arrange the files on his desk. He caressed her hand. She was startled and moved away from the desk.

He slammed his hand on the desk and she reared up in shock,

"answer me."

"I am sorry sir, I did not want to come because…" she was quiet and looked at the door.

"What, tell me?"

"I did not like what you did the last time."

"Oh, I see. You were scared I would make advances at you?"

"Yes sir, you invaded my privacy while I took a bath in your guest bathroom. I did not like the way you touched my boobs."

His angry face softened. "You did not like it?"

"Yes sir, I will not come to your house any more to sleep over and do any work. Please, all official assignments should end in the office."

"Jane, I have this powerful attraction towards you. You hold a special place in my heart. I want to make you the Madam of my house. You would like to be the Madam, right?" He laughed.

"No, I do not want it because that is the same way you have asked every other woman in the office to be your Madam. Are we all very special to you? How many of us will you make the woman of your house?"

"Who told you that rubbish? Hold on, have you women been gossiping about me in this office?"

"No."

"Say the truth. From your gossipy lips, I can tell you are lying," he was a bit scared to what extent the women had exchanged information.

"Nobody told me anything. I am not blind. I saw various sizes of used pants in your bathroom." The Chief Editor shifted uncomfortably in his seat. "The other day; I slept over at your house because there was really much work to do. That was the first and it would be last. I will not condone such rubbish."

He slammed the desk, "mind the audacity of your language."

"You should mind the audacity of your actions! Some female employees are planning to ruin you. They have a video of you forcing yourself on the Secretary while she struggled. There is also a tape recorder in which you threatened to fire the Crime Reporter if she refused to suck your balls."

"Oh, my God, how do you know all these? I cannot believe I am in the dark," he was sweating profusely.

"I am your Personal Assistant; I watch your back, side and front. I am privy to this little information," she raised her index finger and smirked, "so my dear, Chief Editor, let us be professional. My little advice to you is to be humble. One more nonsense move from you, these girls will bring your reputation to dust. I also will, because this very conversation is on record." She fingered her pen recorder, "is there anything else you would like me to take care of, sir? It is time for lunch break."

"Nothing, that will be all," he stuttered. He took some money from his shirt pocket, "here is money for lunch." Jane refused the money and walked out of the office.

The Chief Editor shuddered. He thought about Kola and called him to resume work. "I will practice media with utmost professionalism. I do not want to be limited. The press is a free mouthpiece of the people and a tool for social justice. We protect these ruthless perpetrators while the victims suffer. I stand for equity. I am a Citizen Journalist and I shall stay true to the fairness of media profession. Bye sir," Kola hung the call.

The Chief Editor bowed his head in frustration. He was scared Kola also had some evidence against him.

Eleven

Ase Obi Palaver

James was busy with some paperwork. Anne seductively sat on his laps, "baby, my sweetheart. I need some money to go shopping with my friends," James was mute. Anne rubbed his chest, "Babe, you would give me some money to go shopping, please."

"You will bear for now, I do not have money."

"What should I do when my friends are trying out clothes at the boutique? Did you also forget Toyin's wedding is coming up? I need to buy the attire for the ceremony."

"You can admire and tell them how beautiful they look in the dresses? As for Toyin's wedding, you can wear one of your beautiful dresses."

She got up abruptly, "why are you so stingy? Please, I really need money to shop for some dresses."

"I have lost my job and instead of you to console me, you are adding more stress to my life."

"Are you serious that you will not give me money for shopping?

James, do you know what this means. It means you cannot take care of my needs."

"Baby, please calm down. Why are you being so insensitive? I have just lost my job. Have I ever failed to provide anything you ask for?"

She faced the wall, "that is because I only ask for little things that your entire bank account can afford."

That statement hurt James. "Listen sweetheart, you have to stop acting childish. Anne, if you cannot do anything other than sulk around me, then please leave, I want you out of my sight," Anne looked at him in shock, "drop my spare key on the table, and please close the door behind you."

She pointed a warning finger at him, "James, if I walk out the door, I am never coming back into your life."

"Oh, please, do me that honour, quickly," he bowed to her.

"I do not know why I am still here when there are series of men out there that will give me their ATM cards to go shopping. Worthy men that will pamper me with everything I want and not a stingy man like you. I am bored with you anyway, so I am leaving." She admired her fine polished nails.

"Then do yourself the pleasure. All you have in your brain is your womanly endowments and nothing else. For us to have sex, you must first get a credit alert on your phone. Because of your materialistic nature, I have not been able to make meaningful savings. Ever since we started dating, I have not had good financial direction. All my earnings have just gone down the drain." He clasp his hands, "Please, take your basket self out of my house, and out of my life for good."

James outburst horrified her. She balled her fist, "you are just a broke man. You will not get any girl that can roll on your waist as well as I do on bed," she stormed off. Anne gathered her clothes and accessories in the bedroom; she dragged her box in front of him. "I hate you!" She screamed in his face. She walked out and slammed the door. James covered his ears when she frustratingly screamed in the veranda, "I hate you so much!" He smiled and shook his head exasperatingly. He received an interview message and smiled.

"Toyin, do you really mean that?" Eniola clapped her hands in awe and sat closer to her friend.

"Eniola, believe me. I am not selling ase obi-uniformed attire for my wedding."

"Girl, that sounds ridiculous. Everybody chooses a particular clothe for his or her nuptial celebration."

"Not everybody does that. I will not. Look at these colours," Toyin showed her some colour combination on her phone, "the colour for the day will be purple and gold."

"It is beautiful. We should hit the stores and pick out apparels to sell. George Wrapper will be for parents, Lace and Ankara for guests as well as ase obi girls-traditional wedding escorts."

"No, we are not going anywhere. I mean what I said, Eniola. My prospective wedding guests will shop for their own fabric. That is if they do not already have the dress colour code in their collection of clothes."

"Why do I get the feeling your marriage ceremony will be boring?"

"No, it cannot be boring. No Eniola, not when we have beautiful colours for the day. The hall decorations will be white and gold, the seats covering will be exquisite, look at the hall preview."

Eniola looked at the hall setting on Toyin's phone. She nodded at the spectacular concept. "But Toyin, I cannot imagine a wedding without the bride selling ase obi. Am I unfortunate to be your friend?"

Toyin laughed hilariously, "I too, I was freaked about ase obi until last month. At Janet's wedding, something bothered me a lot. Do you know why Jessica did not attend Janet's wedding?"

"No, that reminds me. Why did she not attend the wedding? She was not even present at the engagement ceremony. She marked her pre-attendance on our online discussion platform, and we did not see her shadow. Hmmm, after all the bragging, she did not turn up. She is just a big girl with small guts," Eniola said and laughed mockingly.

"That is not it, Eniola. Her absence was inevitable. The cost of Janet's ase obi was outrageous, and do not forget Jessica's salary was delayed; she could not buy the attire and other jewelries to compliment the style she chose. I do not want to inconvenience anybody for my wedding. I am quite sure some people have the colour of attire I have chosen. These ase obi colours are recycled; I have many wears with touch of gold and purple. I assumed others do too."

"But Toyin, the design patterns are different."

"My guests can also get the best purple and gold designs they can afford. We really do not have to choose or decide what texture, quality and design pattern a number of people should wear for a ceremony. They should just wear anything they like and can afford. I do not want to inconvenience anybody, really."

"Hmmm, I do not understand you. Wait until the girls hear what your plans are, they will freak out. As for me, I will add a touch of another colour to this dress code, anything to make me look different from the others," Eniola stood and majestically walked back and forth.

"Wear anything you like, my dear friend. The main goal is coming to felicitate with my future husband and I."

Toyin videoed her demonstration. She modeled for more captures. Eniola pulled her high heel shoes and massaged her feet, "Toyin, please transfer the videos to my phone."

"Yes, the media files will flood your device soon. I am sending to your Messenger."

"So, since you are breaking the ase obi rules. I am sure you will not have a pre-wedding shoot."

Toyin covered her mouth in feign shock. "Oh, you say what? Please, do not even joke with that aspect. A picture says more than a thousand words. That is where we are going to pump some good money. We really, really need professional photography and good video coverage to capture the beautiful moments in my married life! It is necessary. I cannot wait to pose for the camera, pre and after my wedding. I am thinking of a cool venue for the shoot."

"There is this new hotel. It is the latest in town."

"No, I do not want anything flashy; I just need a serene environment, probably a waterfall or fountain-a natural setting. Do not worry. We will come up with something."

"You don't want anything flashy? That is another shocker! Your fiancé has money. Babe, please let us spend this money, you will not have your wedding twice. Get off the low horse you are riding and let us paint the town red." Eniola jumped on her seat in excitement.

"Eniola, there are more discussions for another day. Henry has promised to expand my business after the wedding. I do not want anything lavish that will swallow our money."

"Toyin, is it 'our money', or his money?"

"Babe, it is our money o. My traditional marriage was last week, so I am married. I can move into my husband's house without a church wedding. My husband has paid my bride price in full. My parents have given their blessings before God and man."

"Toyin, these your plans are somehow o. Why am I still sitting here? I should go get you some drugs. I think you have a high fever," Eniola touched Toyin's forehead, "you are fine, but we need to get your head re-examined. Oh, I think you are losing it. Anyway, we must have a white wedding. Do not even joke with that, you cannot take all the fun from us. Just stop being selfish."

"Babe, is it your marriage plans?"

"It is my best friend's marriage plans," Eniola hit her with a throw pillow and they played around. The doorbell rang. They stopped the chase.

Anne walked in with a sullen face. "Hi Eniola, hello bride to be," she flopped into a chair and exhaled.

"Anne, what is the matter with you?" Toyin asked.

"It looks like her boyfriend has broken up with her," Eniola smirked.

"Stop the joke, Eniola. This is not funny, Anne looks sad."

"She is right. James broke up with me," Anne hid her face in her dress and cried. Eniola and Toyin came over to her side with consoling words and hugs. Anne narrated what transpired between her and James.

Eniola gave Toyin an, *I told you look.*

Toyin patted Anne's hand, "stop crying, Anne. I know James did not mean it."

"No, it is over between us." Anne said.

"I know you do not mean it too. You love each other very much. You breathe for each other, what makes you think the two of you can live apart," Toyin said.

"I mean it. James really hurt me with the way he treated me. Just because he lost his job, he refused to give me some money. He has never done that before. Maybe there is another girl in his life."

"I don't think he has any other intimate girlfriend," Toyin said.

"Then why else was he so mean to me?"

"Every human has a limit to what they can endure. I know you Anne; your words would have been awful. He lost his job for goodness sakes. The least you could do was encourage him. But no, you nagged him for money. Anne, that was insensitive," Toyin said.

"Do not worry girl, you will get a new man," Eniola said

Anne's shoulder slumped, "but finding a good man is not easy! After I left his house, I immediately accepted a date from one of my admirers. This man has been asking me out for over a year. Could you believe, he met me at a park instead of the restaurant I suggested. Do you know he did not give me transport money back to my house?"

"So, did you trek back home?" Eniola tried to muffle a jeering laughter.

"No, thank God I had money in the house. I took a cab because I had just a Hundred Naira on me. I paid the Taxi Driver with my last money. Now I am so broke I do not know what to do. All these toasters are monsters up front."

"No, the kinds of toasters you meet are beasts. Speak for yourself and leave other people's toasters out of it," Eniola said.

"I feel James is the best. He would have ridden me on his back if there were no vehicles in the world. I miss him," Anne said dreamily.

Eniola and Toyin's laugher brought her back from the fantasy world.

Toyin gloated, "I said it; she is going back to her dream man. She would be like, *James, I prepared your favourite meal, baby will you forgive me, I am sorry for my rude and insensitive behaviour.*" Eniola and Toyin laughed.

Anne scowled, "You know me so well, eh." Eniola told Anne all about the wedding plans. "Oh, Toyin, I am so relieved. I thought of leaving town for a while because I may not be able to afford your ase obi. James had reprimanded me before he gave me money for Janet's ase obi, of which she is yet to give me gift for buying her costume.

I am sure she had used the profit from the ase obi sales to arrange her marriage. I hope it does not take her months to give us gifts for buying the attire. Her ase obi was very expensive, and so I thought you might want to surpass her price listing. Thank you for these sensible arrangements.

We should go back to how marriage preparations panned out in the past. Our mothers did not have hypertension when they got wedding invites because they had wardrobes for different occasions.

If I had known you were not selling ase obi for your wedding, I would have simply asked James to give me money to buy a gift item. We would never have had that quarrel," said Anne.

Eniola gave Anne *you are such a bore* look.

Toyin cleared her throat, "Anne, please do not be offended, I want to say this as a good friend."

"Yes go on, Toyin, you are a sensible friend, unlike Eniola who delights in mocking me." Eniola hit Anne with a pillow and Anne playfully nudged her head.

"I hope this does not sound like a mockery. Anne, I think eh, you should dust your certificate and go out to seek employment."

"Toyin…My dear friend, you do not have to tell me. I have sent my CV to some firms. I hope I get a job soon."

"That is good. So in the meantime, you can join me in the printing press," Toyin said.

"No Toyin, I need a job that I would be paid. I do not want Madam and Apprentice activity. I do not have time for apprenticeship. I need to make money."

"I will pay you. You will work as a paid intern."

Anne was confused, "But I cannot even operate a copier. What will you pay me to do?"

"I will pay you to learn graphic designs, build media contents and other related art, you will learn general printing. I will pay you to boost your interest. You will amass great skills. You will be empowered to fend for yourself. We will work together until your job application clicks. Okay?"

Anne nodded excitedly, "Thank you Toyin, you are being sensible, so sensible that I agree to all your wedding plans and arrangements. I think Janet is not talking to Jessica because Jessica did not buy her ase obi. I did not dance very well at the wedding reception because I still owed her money for the ase obi. Some expenses are unnecessary. I did not have peace of mind until I paid her the money."

"Yes, some obligations are not necessary. We can forgo some and do the most important," Toyin said.

"Toyin, to avoid unnecessary expenses, I suggest you have your honeymoon in your matrimonial home," Eniola said.

"Now you are thinking more than I am, it seems you have a very high fever. I want my wedding night to be special; I do not trust this electricity supplier. While we will be busy making a baby, there might be power outage. Who will get up to turn on the lousy generator? The air conditioner has to be on because we will be doing very hot stuffs in the room," Toyin said and giggled.

"You are a bad babe...so hot." Eniola grinned and threw a pillow at Toyin.

"Well, I think it will be wise if newlyweds consummate their marriage on matrimonial bed. I mean, all kinds of bodies have lain on those hotel beds," Anne said.

"Hmmm, I think I will arrange with the hotel to allow us bring our mattress and bed sheet." Toyin said. They all laughed.

On Toyin's wedding day, she received many wedding largesse. Friends and relatives shared souvenirs to guests.

Toyin thanked her aunt for the wedding gift she presented. "Toyin my dear, I was able to save money and make souvenirs because you did not sell ase obi. I had the particular colours you picked as your dress code. God bless your union and bless you with more wisdom my dear." They hugged and pecked one another on the cheeks.

The couple opened the dance floor and guests joined the wedding merriment.

Twelve

Ama and Amber

It was a hazy evening. Ama, my roommate and I prepared noodle and egg for dinner. We shared a studio flat. We were eating late because I had expected pastries from an admirer. After the meal, we sat on the cool floor. I put on the radio. It screeching sound made my ears cringe.

"Amber, put off that damn radio," Ama said.

"I wanted to hear some songs."

"But the radio was screechy like a witch cry."

"I could have tuned the radio until I got a better frequency. It is a boring evening. There is no battery power on my laptop and I doubt if the Electricity Company will restore power tonight. We could pass time with some cool music. Come on, Ama, it is Friday." I tuned the radio.

"It is useless," Ama snatched the radio and removed the battery. "That's it." She breathed deeply. "Amber, please let us have some peace. Do not bore me with this grumpy old radio. I am still irritated with your boyfriend."

"He is not my boyfriend," I collected the radio and placed it on my reading table. "We cannot even get along as friends."

Ama joked about the 'boyfriend' that had brought two apples for me. The banker insisted to see me. I did not want to go out, he opted to come to the house, and I told him to get snacks for us.

"You are the apple of my eyes. These apples are the symbol of my love," Ama mimicked his words.

"Ama, you had better stop fooling around. I did not find it funny. He made me felt my worth was two greenish apples."

"I felt pity you had to listen to his boring talks. His wooing method was tasteless and tactless. What does he really want from you, a dummy? He just did all the talking and expected you to accept his arrogant courtship proposal. I am glad you declined."

"I felt like stuffing the apples in his mouth. I cannot wait for tomorrow so that we will go to buy some snacks. This illness has left me in a bad state. My mouth taste bitter from the malaria, and his actions made it worse," we laughed.

Our laughter died when we heard the cringing sound of a gong, like one beaten in a village shrine. The sound clung twice and we hugged each other. "Amber, what is that sound? It is frightening." Ama wound her hands tightly around my neck.

"Get your hands off me, you are going to choke me, fool!" She let go and squirmed.

"That sound. It sent chills down my spine. What was that?"

I massaged my neck. "I do not know. The sound is so horrid." A male and female exchanged inaudible words. I began to shiver.

Ama doused the candle quickly. She peeped outside through a small opening on the iron door and saw a lantern burning low, "they are sitting right outside our veranda. It seems they are going to use us for sacrifices. A red clothe is tied to the lantern. Oh, we are dead. Amber, I warned we should not rent this house. The neighbourhood looks creepy. It looks haunted. Oh, who will rescue us? Oh, Lord, in this time I call on you to save your children. Oh, Lord, send your Angels to protect us. I promise I will never sin again. I will never mock anybody," Ama poured anointing oil on the apples. She knelt and prayed silently on the apples.

I grabbed my phone to call our boss, "hello sir, please can you send the Army to our neighbourhood? I think we are in grave danger, some people are trying to kill us."

"Hello Amber, I cannot hear you. What did you say or do I call back. Hang up I will call," he cut the call while I was still talking.

I was typing a text message to him when my phone turned off. We were doomed. Ama's phone was also off. We raised our mattress and lay underneath. None of us knew what was in each other's mind. I said my last prayers.

I felt liquid touch my feet. I did not realise I urinated on my body. The liquid was very cold while my body temperature was hot. I doubted and kicked Ama because it might be her urine.

As feet stepped on our veranda, we became more frightened,

"Amber, I think they are coming for us. We are going to die! Oh, God, please receive our poor souls," I said. We just lay beneath the mattress and expected the worse.

I opened my eyes and saw Ama soundly asleep on the mattress. I wondered if heaven had our kind of mattress. I rubbed my eyes. The environment was the same setting as our room. I tapped her, "wake up, Ama," she grumbled and rolled off the mattress to the floor. I unlocked the door and slowly pushed it open.

The usual morning activities were before my eyes. I thought heaven was not different from earth. I sighed and drew the curtains. I thought this was a lower heaven. Maybe God did not take us to a better place because we mocked the Banker. However, this place was still amazing; I had my room and my best friend.

The Nurse in my neighbourhood greeted, "Teacher, good morning o." She walked passed with her children. I came out and saw two Okada men-motorcyclists fighting over a keg. A cock chased a wild hen and pounced on her.

"Teacher, you are just waking up? This long vacation is good for your body o. Good morning," a female hawker said. She smiled and called out her wares '*buy your sweet bitter leaf and fresh tomatoes.*'

I turned around and kicked Ama. She got up and grabbed me, "where are we? Where are we?" She tried to get under the mattress.

I shook her roughly, "wake up; I think we are in heaven. We made it to heaven, we are not burning in hell," Ama became calm. She looked around and smiled happily.

Few minutes later, our Property Owner called out to us, "Amber! Ama! Where are these girls? Pay up your rent, please. You said you will pay by month end, and this is the first day of December."

Ama and I rolled our eyes. "Well, I do not think we made it to heaven," Ama said.

We took the back door and saw the Property Owner standing with a receipt booklet and a big padlock in his hands.

"Landlord, you are here. What are you doing here?" I asked.

"You are asking what the owner of this property is doing here. Have I trespassed on my own land? Did you forget my family and I also live in this compound or you are out of your mind? Please, I came for my money, go in, and arrange for the remaining six months' rent." He sat at our entrance and shook his legs in agitation.

Ama looked confused, "Amber, do you think the Landlord is God?"

"Then I think we are not in the right place. Just get the money so that he may return to hell and leave the heaven peacefully."

The Property Owner stared at us as if we were crazy. We found out it was a vigilante raucous we heard last night. It was a usual way to guard the environment in the month of December.

A male and female usually take turn and sit out to keep vigil. We missed the information because we never attended tenants' meetings, and did not tune in to the radio to have caught the general announcement.

Thirteen

The Ugly Side of Motherhood

Caleb spilled palm oil on the kitchen floor. Rachael was enraged, "oh, all my morning of cleaning and dusting is a waste. How will I mop and prepare dinner in time before your father's arrival?" she spanked him on his buttocks and dragged him out of the house. "If you think I am going to spare you today, then you should cease to call me mother. Woe betides a child that will make me labour endlessly. As if doing regular chores are not enough, you will give me more task when it is time for me to have some rest."

"Please mommy, let me go. Please do not punish me; I will be a good boy. Do not lock me up in the darkroom. I hate it in the dark room. I get so scared. Daddy has said you should never lock me up again."

"Yes, he is your sweet daddy and I am the bad mommy, eh. I have told him to take you along to his office. He decided you should stay home today for a little body temperature you had. I know you faked it, you were not sick. You just did not want to go to school so that you can make my life a living hell. Your father let you stay because he is not the one to face such mess. I will lock you up. When he comes back, he can come and play the hero and a good father. Right now, I need some semblance of sanity around my house because you are driving me crazy." She opened the garage and dumped him on a sack of sawdust.

Caleb pounded on the door with his fists, calling and crying out to his mother to bring him out, "I am sorry mommy, please let me out. I promise to be a good boy, please let me out of here." He severely hit the door.

The Gateman was sympathetic towards the child. He went close to the door and stole glances at the house. Rachael was nowhere in sight. He tiptoed to the garage. He was about to open the door when a tennis ball missed his head and hit the garage' window.

Rachael shouted at him, "If you dare open that door, I will fire you in an instant and do not think your boss will get you back on the job this time."

He stood at attention, "yes ma, and pardon me. I am sorry. His tears upset me. I cannot stand it. It is not fair how you treat your son. He is only seven year old. Please, give him a lesser punishment. He can kneel in front of you. Ma, you torture him emotionally too. I pray he should not hurt himself one day."

Rachael rushed out of the house, "will you keep shut? Shut your stupid mouth. Is he your child? Oh, I see you want to lecture me on how to raise my child. I should leave him to become wayward and tomorrow he becomes a nuisance, the society blames me. They will say the woman did not train up her child well."

"Ma, please, you misunderstand me, I am only saying…"

"Oh, just shut up! Shut up! I can see you are jobless. I do not see your need in this house. My husband just wastes monthly salary on you and you feed fat from my kitchen. In fact, get into the house," she started towards the house.

He remained standing, "you say what?"

She turned around, "I said get into the house immediately," she came forward and dragged him by his ears, "have you gone deaf? I said get into the house. You have the guts to stand there and exchange words with me. You will see what I will do to you today. You will use your tongue to mop the floor. You love my son more than me, right. You shall clean up this mess. Get into the house quickly."

The Gateman followed her into the house. He mopped the floor thoroughly with an old towel. "Ma, I am done. Please, will you let your son out now?"

"I will release him when I want to. You are even better off as a houseboy than a gateman; you are just useless at the gatepost. I will speak to my husband when he returns. You will take up housework as well."

"Okay ma," he smiled happily.

"I will not add a penny to your salary."

"Oh, madam, I will be taking up more tasks. It is not fair to pay me a salary for two jobs."

"I do not care. You can use the gate; nobody is begging you to stay here. There are many people looking for this job offer."

"I am sorry ma, the pay is fair enough," he bowed.

"Good…Now take yourself out of my kitchen. Go to the living room, there is some money on the table, go and get me a large size of pizza. Make sure my money does not miss from that table. I know the serial numbers on those notes by heart."

He looked offended, "Madam I am not a thief."

"Oh, shut up and move."

He came back to the kitchen, "Madam, please do you have Hundred Naira? I want to use it to take a bike transport."

"You mean you do not have change in your pocket?"

"No madam, it is One Thousand Naira note I have."

She clapped her hands, "Oho, I said it; you are really a Big Boy-rich man. My husband just pays you for nothing. Give me all the money on you," he gave back the money for the pizza, "Idiot I mean all the money in your pocket."

"Madam, this is not fair." She slapped him on the face and snapped her fingers at him. He gave her all his money.

"Now go and get my pizza," she took a seat, "you will walk back and forth to the mall. Do not let my pizza grow cold. Touch your feet to your head in a race to come back quickly." He bowed and hurried out of the house. Rachael put on the television; she was excited watching a music video.

On his way out, the Gateman called out, "Caleb, I will be back soon.

I will plead with your mommy to let you out, okay?"

"Okay Uncle," Caleb faintly said.

The Gateman borrowed money from an Orange Seller and took a cab to the mall. It was a 'one chance' cab-the cab driver and the passengers were thieves. They robbed and dropped him in the middle of the road.

He panicked and put his hands on his head and thought how a stranded man could get a hot pizza. He thought Rachael may skin him alive if he came back empty handed. His rescue would be to visit his benevolent boss at the office. He trekked to the office.

* * * * * *

He reached the office and told his boss everything. "You mean you walked all the way from the house to my office?" His boss asked.

"Yes sir, please give me money to buy pizza for madam, you will deduct it from my salary. Please help me out, sir."

The boss hit his knuckles on the table in contemplation, "it is okay, there would be no need to deduct it from your salary. Please, put my bag in the car and wait for me," the Gateman took the bag. He remained standing, "I said you should go and sit in the car. I will tidy some things and be with you in ten minutes. We will buy the pizza and go home together."

"Okay sir, thank you," he walked away relieved.

* * * * * *

They reached home and the Gateman came down from the car to open the gates. Rachael rushed out of the house. "Oh, darling, you are back so early. Were you missing me? I miss you so much." She hugged and gave him a peck. Her husband held her waist possessively. He kissed her passionately.

The Gateman giggled and looked away shyly. He retrieved two packs of pizza from the back seat.

She pointed a finger at the Gateman, "you got me two packs of pizza? Why? I gave you money for one. I hope you have not stolen my money?"

Her husband loosened his grip on her, "honey, calm down. I bought one for you and the other is for our son. Let us go in. I am hungry. Where is my son?"

The Gateman looked at Rachael. She was silent for a while, "he is in the garage," she said.

Her husband was shocked. "Have I not warned you never to lock him up again? You locked him up in that old garage. Rachael, have you forgotten our son is asthmatic?"

Rachael gasps, "my God. I forgot." She covers her mouth.

"Move aside," he pushed her away and walked to the garage. He opened it and found their son dead.

Fourteen

Nome and the Custom of Vabam

Nome sat on a low stool. She fingered her bracelet, made from tiny seashells. She had lived with her aunt who was a renowned fisherwoman in Kopi.

The reason her parents summoned her back to Vabam sounded ridiculous to her. The flaming lantern centred on her beautiful oval face. Nome's mother had been unsuccessful to convince her to accept the marriage between herself and her sister's ex-husband.

Her father tried to make her understand the import of her action, "this has never happened in our clan. Asoka wants to ruin our reputation. You will have to go in order to wipe away the shame your sister has dusted on our image. Nome, you are our redeemer."

"I wish you did not ask this of me. Father, how can I take over my sister's husband? Please, I will not be able to stomach that, the thought alone is repulsive to me. I will not be able to do it," Nome said.

"You can my daughter, and it is for our best interests," her father said.

"What about my interest? Nobody cares about my feelings."

"We do, that is why you will fill in for your sister. Our custom demands such duty from us. Your action will redeem your image as well. It is for the best interest of the Manzeem household. The reclamation of our clan's image rests on your shoulder," he said.

"Father, he called my sister trash. What makes you all think I will not be a bag of dirt in his house?"

"You are not like your younger sister. Asoka is a mess, she has always been flirtatious, but we thought it was an unusual aura during puberty, and it will automatically turn off when she settles down with a man. Sadly, your mother and I got it wrong. Now shame smiles at our huts, our roof will not stand for long if you do not raise it by fulfiling this custom. Nome, my lovely daughter, you will have to go and redeem our pride. I know you will make a good wife. He will wish he plucked you first rather than your sister. I am sure that if you had been around when he came knocking at our garden, he would have opted to tend you instead, my beautiful flower."

"Father, you're flattering me. You are not making me feel any better."

"I cannot pacify you. I would not even try to. I have only told you the truth. I never chose a favourite out of my children. I will not do that now."

"Father, this is not right."

"Tradition is right, our ancestors are not wrong. Vabam stands still because it holds its customs closely to heart. Norms and values is what keep a society in the light. Look at your mother; she is a replacement of her elder sister who ran away with her lover. I rejected your mother when she came to be my wife. I was very hurt. My wife's betrayal hurt me so much. I hated the home she came from, but I had to fulfil these traditions. I faulted everything around me, but after I got hold of my emotions, I did accept your mother, because tradition is right. I was a happier man with your mother. She showered me with love and devotion. I fell in love again. Perhaps, this will be your fate, or greater than ours," love for each other sparkled in her parents' eyes.

"My daughter, at least just meet him. You might like him," Nome's mother prodded into the discussion.

"Mother, I find this distasteful; you people should not make me do this. How can I bed my sister's husband? He is my sister's husband."

"If that is what is bothering you, know that the moment your sister disobeyed the laws of marriage. You automatically became his bride," her mother was happy to stream this information.

They were silent. The lamp burned low and supplied less light to the hut. "Okay, I will think about it," Nome said. They nodded. Nome bid her parents good night and went to her room.

She could not sleep. She tossed on the bed, "I cannot do this," she stood up and pace about the room, "why should I bear the consequences of someone's action. Asoka will be happy wherever she is with her lover, while I will face the hate from her husband. What is the guarantee that he will treat me right? Will he have an iota of respect for me?

Mother may be lucky father found love with her, he respects her but that is her luck, and my case may be different. I cannot stand this humiliation."

She packed her clothes in a box and went to her parents' room. They were sound asleep. She touched their feet and placed the hand on her forehead; tears filled her eyes as she turned away from them. Nome ran away.

Nome's decision was an abomination. Nobody trounce this law of Vabam. Her parents and all members of each clan faced cold-shouldering from the society people.

The king ruled that no daughter born in the respective households of Nome's parents would receive bride price. Any suitor could take them home without performing formal marital rites. Bachelors of repute did not come to knock on their doors.

One year later, Nome was cohabiting with her lover in another village. They were very much in love. The man decided to come and see her parents to fulfil formal marriage rites. She brought him home. Her lover turned out to be her sister's husband.

Fifteen

Anita is in the Dark

I went to buy some provisions at a regular store. The Shop Owner was sad. Her teenage daughter was bartering words with her. The girl demanded money for unnamed items and the mother did not oblige her.

"Anita, you will not get any money until you tell me what it is meant for. I have paid your fees. All your books and wears are complete, you have food to eat, what else do you need? Tell me. I will either buy it or give you the money if it is something you can buy by yourself."

She hissed at her mother and stormed out of the shop. I wanted to talk to the girl but I decided another day would be good.

On my way home, I saw a woman waved Anita to come over. "It was very good of you to challenge your mother. She has the money and does not want to give you because she is stingy. Your mother is wicked. I told you, she does not care about you. Do you know what next to do?" Anita shook her head, "okay. You will apologize to your mother. She will forgive you and allow you stay in her shop. Once you get possession of her coffer, take some money, and bring it to me. I will help you save the money. Any time you need the money to buy anything, I will give you the money," the woman said.

Anita was happy over the mischief. I tried to see the woman's face but it was too dark. A car headlight shone on her face. I saw it was their neighbour. The woman had had a fight with Anita's mother over business-she accused Anita's mother of stealing some of her customers. It just happened that the woman was very rude and her nonchalant attitude towards sales drove her first-time buyers away.

I shook my head as I walked home. Gone were the days that random African parents were guardians of any child. Any kind elder was the disciplinarian of a child. These days, some adults just watch them go astray and expose the child to wayward lifestyle.

A month later, I was polishing my nails at the big market when Anita and her friends passed by. They were chatting and laughing. She was in the company of two junior students and three senior students from her school.

Anita was a junior student. They bought some clothes at a stall next to the nail technician's kiosk. I could not conceal my shock when I saw most of the girls, including Anita, pay with wad of naira notes. How did they come in possession of such amount of money and go unnoticed in school.

I remembered back in primary school. I had taken money from my mother's purse. My teacher saw I was buying more pastries than my pocket money could afford. She called me aside and asked where I got extra money. She dipped her hands into my pocket and found bigger amount of money. I told her my mother had given me the money to purchase fish after close hours.

She accompanied me home to verify my claims. When we got home, I stared timidly at my mother, with my eyes, I pleaded with her to admit anything my teacher asked.

My mother told her she had given me the money to buy fish from the market. My teacher apologised for the inconvenience. She took it upon herself to shop for it. She took the money and went to the market. She returned with five big fishes.

My mother prepared it with enough pepper and gave me to eat. She sat beside me with a slim long cane until I finished eating the last morsel of fish. I overfed and slept on the spot. At midnight, my mother woke me up and flogged me mercilessly. She beat out all the protein from my body. From that day, I promised never to take anything that was not mine.

Their shopping bag was full with party clothes. The Nail Technician affirmed the girls were regular patrons. She had fixed their eyelashes and nails on three occasions. She disclosed Anita just recently became friends with the unprincipled girls.

Anita gave the clothes to one of her friends to keep in her house, "my mother will make a scene if she sees this kind of clothes with me. I will change in your house before we leave for any party."

In the evening, I went to the shop to buy bread. "Anita, I am not happy with the way you spoke to your mother that day. That was rude," I said.

She shoved the bread into my hands and demanded for the money. I paid her and walked away. I will talk to her some other day. First, I will tell her mother who her enemy was.

Sixteen

Give Me a Grandchild

Donald's mother arrived from the village. "You will not marry her. If you go against my wish, then you should also make arrangements for my burial ceremony," she said. He looked at her with plea in his eyes, "I will be dead the day you take her as wife." Donald was speechless.

After a while, he spoke, "Mama, I am helpless. You are not making things easy for me. What should I tell Jessica? Mama please, have a rethink, this is not fair. Would you wish such a thing is done to your own daughter?"

"My daughter would heed my words. I took Jessica as my daughter. She was your fiancée, after all."

"She is still my fiancée, Mama."

"Was, I said she was. You are not going to marry that girl. It will be over my dead body. Ten years ago, I encouraged the two of you to get married. You were a bull and she was pig-headed. You wanted time to expand your business, and she was busy building her future, her career is still a priority. For three months now, she has been away on a business trip, and you are here stupidly thinking she is ready to settle down any time soon. The two of you have what you desire. Now, it is my turn to do and have what I have always wanted. Adaobi," she called. A young girl walked into the house, "come and sit by me," the girl sat next to her. She patted her back, "this is the girl I have found for you, I have paid her bride price. She is your wife."

"Why did you do that? No, this is preposterous. How can you do this without my consent? Mama, you should not have done this, this is not right."

"What is the matter? Is she not beautiful? Stand up my beautiful girl; let him see what I paid for. Go in front of your husband. Turn around and let him see how lovely you are." The girl turned sideways, front and back. Donald salivated at her luscious form. His mother grinned at him. "My eyesight is very sharp. She is a well-behaved girl, very dutiful and obedient. My son, she is a good home maker that will bear you healthy children and take care of your home."

"Mama, Jessica is not immune to bearing children and taking care of the house."

His mother gave him a stern look, "Adaobi, go into the bedroom, the master's bedroom by the right, it is you and your husband's bedroom. Go and refresh, I am sure your husband will join you soon. Put my bag in the second room."

"Okay, Mama," Adaobi smiled shyly at Donald. She lifted the bag and went in.

"Listen son. This young woman will bear healthy children for you. Jessica's waist will be weak to push in the labour room. She has used all her strength to work. You are old and she is old. Son, you have to be practical. This situation requires wisdom. Adaobi is just seventeen year old. When you live and join your ancestors, she will be very much around and healthy to look after your children. Jessica does not have this vibrancy. She will have complications during pregnancy and after childbirth. Donald, her age is not friendly for a laborious journey. Hmmm, and you, your sperm grows watery too; Jessica has drained all your thickness. She drained them down the sewer." She snorted.

"What kind of talk is that? Stop it, Mama."

"Oh, my son, please give the remaining vitamins to your new wife before that woman who is not ready to settle down finishes it all. It is so unfair you delayed this long to give me grandchildren. At least, give me children; let me carry my grandchildren now that my hands still has strength. Your father's wish was to carry his grandchild before his death. My son, you are the only child I have," she wept. Donald consoled his mother and stared at the ceiling.

✻ ✻ ✻ ✻ ✻ ✻

In the night, Donald made love to Adaobi. A month later, she conceived. Jessica returned from the business trip. Donald was working on his computer.

"Hey honey, I am back!" she hugged and kissed him, "baby, I missed you so much. I wish you had been on this trip with me. We would have had lots of fun, from Texas to New York. The arrangements were awesome."

"I see you had your fun," Donald paused to look at her. "It is obvious. I am glad you did. I thought you would have stayed longer."

"Does that mean you did not miss me? What have you been up to?" She took a bite of his toast and sipped tea, "I see you have been taking good care of yourself. I am confident I can go on a trip and you will be just fine. My baby is so grown," she kissed his cheeks soundly. She flung her jacket on the chair. Jessica wantonly walked towards Donald and shook her cleavages in his face, "sweetheart, what I need right now is a great massage, from my outer to inner body," she kissed his lips, "you know how to do it baby, come on; let us go into the room. I missed you so much, come give it to me baby," she rubbed his crotch with her knee and Donald's penis hardened, "Baby, you have not said anything. You missed me speechless, right. I will show you some new moves in the bedroom."

"That is what you know best. Look at her," Donald's mother hissed. Jessica hastily grabbed her jacket. She wore it and dressed up properly.

"Mama, you are home? Welcome Mama, when did you arrive? You are looking so beautiful, well taken care of," Jessica was nervous. *'Oh, why did Donald not tell me Mama was around? I will have a dose of backlashing today.'* Jessica thought. She straightened her dress and smiled.

"I have been around for centuries. Good to know you noticed I am looking well taken care of." Jessica nodded nervously. Mama called out, "Adaobi, please serve my breakfast and bring my medicine box."

Jessica adjusted her clothes and coughed. Mama ogled at her for a while and focused on the television. Adaobi came with a tray of breakfast.

Jessica's eyes fell on her three-month-old baby bump. She said, "Hi," Adaobi smiled politely, "you must be Donald's relation." Mama looked at Jessica scornfully. Jessica turned to Donald, "sweetheart, who is this girl?"

"I will tell you," Mama said and stood to take the tray from Adaobi, "this beautiful pregnant girl is my son's wife."

Jessica was shocked. She angrily faced Donald. "Baby, I cannot explain," Donald said and raised his hands.

"What do you mean you cannot explain? Between you and your mother, who is the joker here?" Donald looked away, "look at me Donald. I am talking to you!"

"Did you hear the woman you wanted to marry, call me a joke? She is rude to your mother and you just sit there and do nothing. Anyway, I am so glad she did not turn out to be my daughter-in-law. She would have beaten me to death while you stand and enjoy the show."

"Mama, what do you want me to do? She only asked a question," Donald said.

"She has bewitched you. Let us leave," She took Adaobi's hand and led her into the bedroom.

"Donald, what is going on here? Answer me and do not sit there as if you have suddenly gone dumb."

"Jessica, Mama married that girl for me."

"Did your meddling mother sex her? You married while I was away. For just six months I was away, you stabbed me in the back so much it pieced my heart," she knelt before him, "Donald, please tell me this is all a lie, it will hurt me too much."

"Jessica, I was patiently waiting for your return, but Mama came along," he pointed towards the hallway, "Adaobi is my wife."

"You now comfortably address her as your wife. You bedded her while professing love to me all these days. How could you Donald?"

"She is my wife, and the mother of my unborn baby. I was waiting for you but Mama came along. She threatened me with her life. I had to fulfil my duty as a son. Mama's action is not that bad either. I have been seeing the good side of it. Adaobi is a lovely sweet girl. She has been a great wife. Jessica, somehow I wish you remained abroad; maybe a greater promotion or something to keep you there. I would have had a valid excuse to call off our relationship. I guess, I was just waiting for an opportunity to get married. You were always postponing our wedding. I am not young any more. We are not young, Jessica. I wish you all the best." Jessica nodded and left the house.

Donald broke into tears. His mother patted his back, "my son, it was for the best."

"Mama, there was so much hurt in her eyes. I am pained Mama, how could I have done that to my love, Jessica."

"Son, it was for the best. Think about it, there will be vibrancy in your home. Adaobi will bear strong children. She would look after you when you are weak. Her strength will double as a mother and father. Do not cry my son; it was for the best Jessica went away. I wish her good luck. I wish she had married you when I pressured her to." Donald cried on her shoulder.

Donald grew fond of his wife. They went out together and had fun. Mama took care of Adaobi, as her pregnancy grew heavier. Donald could not wait to be a great father as he was a dotting husband. Adaobi gave birth to a baby girl. She died few days later from birth delivery complications. Donald did not remarry. Mama took care of the child.

Seventeen

The Wrong Sex Education

Amaya was pregnant. She could feel it. The distressed teenager stayed long in the bathroom, trying to wash off the pregnancy. She scrubbed her body thoroughly with iron sponge.

She cried bitterly. The first day she saw her menstruation, her mother had told her she had grown into a woman. Amaya's mother told her to stay away from the opposite sex, *'If a man touches you, then you will get pregnant.'* Amaya mother's words rang in her ears. She scrubbed her breasts harder.

Amaya had been careful not to be in body contact with any man that was not her relation. Today, a man's hand slightly touched her breast. She had been in a rush to answer her mother's call. Amaya hurriedly tied wrapper over her body.

In her haste, she bumped into a male neighbour. He tried to hold her from falling and accidently touched her breast. Amaya was terrified of what will happen if her mother found out.

Her mother promised to kick her out of the house in a disgraceful style if a man ever touched her. She came out of the bathroom sober.

Amaya wore her clothes. She broke her piggy bank. In tears, Amaya ran away from home with little money.

Eighteen

Shredded

Jami held vegetables in one hand and used the other to play ball. She threw the tennis egg in the air. She rushed forward and caught it before it reached the ground.

Jami was a happy girl who loved to play while on errands. For a task of five minutes, Jami could take over thirty minutes to accomplish it. Her mother had tried to beat and talked her out of the habit, but Jami was Jami. She was so playful she had once lost money for a week's meal.

Some boys were playing football. It rolled toward her feet and she trapped it with a foot. She juggled the ball and kicked it towards the goal post. It was a superb straight goal from the distance she stood. The boys applauded her skills and blew whistles. They asked her to join the game but she declined.

Jami's gaze locked with the Goalkeeper's eyes. He was staring at her in open admiration. He was admiring her bare feet; they were long and finely polished. He raised his head to her face. He stared in awe at her cute face.

The Goalkeeper was her senior in school; he was one year ahead of her. Jami blushed and ran home. The other boys cheered their friend for being besotted with Jami. He ran after her. She stopped and waited shyly for him to speak. He told her he liked her athletic skill. He asked Jami to be his friend and teammate. She agreed and they shook hands.

Jami got home. She was still blushing at the encounter with her new friend. There were guests in the house. They had come to marry Jami. Jami was sad. She went into the kitchen. She sliced the vegetable while crying.

Her mother came into the kitchen. She held Jami's hands, "Jami, do not think we do not love you. Your father and I want the best for you. Altai is a very good man. He will care and provide your needs. We are too poor to give you education. We do not wish to give you out in marriage so early. Right now, neither your father nor I have a Hundred Naira in this house. We can barely feed."

"Mama, I do not want to get married. I want to go to school. I have a dream to become a great scholar and footballer. Someday, I want to marry my prince charming."

"You must stop dreaming so boisterously. Your brothers have to go to school. When you marry Altai, we can use the dowry to send your eldest brother to school. Subsequently, your husband will sponsor your younger brothers through school. Your brothers will be educated and have good jobs. Then, we will be able to break out of poverty."

"Mama, do I not have a right to go to school. Who says a girl cannot dream and have what she wishes for?"

"Who will pay your school fees? Jami, we cannot even afford to buy you sanitary towel."

Jami's father gave her out in marriage to a man of seventy years. She was married at age fourteen. Two months later, Jami got pregnant. During childbirth, her vulva was torn. Her husband took the baby home to his mother. Jami remained in the hospital, bleeding.

There were many teenagers like Jami in that hospital. Their husbands and relatives lacked the funds for surgery. They left them to a bad fate, to bleed and rot. The hospital smelled of their urine.

Two months later, Jami's husband married another wife. He married a girl of eleven years. The society did not criticise his decision because polygamous marriage was acceptable. Society did not reprimand Altai to treat Jami either.

Nineteen

The Masculine Strength of a Woman

Mabel ran into the room crying. Her mother-in-law sadly shook her head, "Did you have to hit her? Tony, it would be of benefit to train Mabel into a strong courageous woman. Instead of trying to break her, why don't you encourage her to be brave?"

"What do you mean? Mama, do you mean my wife should rub shoulder with me. No way, I did not marry my fellow man. She should know her place, I will have her soft and compliant. Mama, how dare she look me in the eyes while I am talking?"

Once again, anger enveloped Tony. He stood and burst into their bedroom. Mabel jostled up and backed into a corner. Her hands shook in fright, warding him off from hitting her again. She hid her face. The warning blow had swelled an eye. He took one malicious look at her and clenched his fist. He stormed out of the bedroom in fury. Mabel fell to the floor crying.

Some minutes later, she heard Tony and Mama's scream. Mabel dried her tears and went to the door. She peeped through the keyhole and saw some armed robbers.

"Please, please do not hurt my family. Do not kill me. I swear I do not have any money," Tony said.

One of the robbers slapped him. He dragged Mama by her neck and pushed her to the floor. Mabel flinched and reversed from the door. She feared they were going to kill all of them in the house. The Informant definitely knew there was a lot of money in Tony's possession. However, he had taken the Five Million Naira to the bank. Mabel started praying.

One of the robbers walked towards the bedroom. Mabel panicked and put the Holy Bible aside. She stood up and got a baton from Tony's sport bag. She hid behind the door. As soon as the thief fully entered the room, she hit him on the head. He dropped to the ground and fell unconscious.

"Mano, Mano, what are you doing? Have you found the money? Hurry up!" The gang leader called out to the unconscious comrade. He walked towards the hallway.

Mabel could not let him come in. She ran out and met him halfway, "he is packing the money. I showed him where the cash and jewels are." He dragged her to the living room. "Please, do not hurt us. You will get the money," she knelt slowly; her hands were behind her back.

He menacingly moved towards Mabel, "keep that gun close to his brain, while I taste his meal," he said to another comrade. Tony shut his eyes and gasped. The gang leader roughly pushed Mabel to the floor. She kept her hands at her back and laid still.

Tony looked helpless. He cursed himself, "damn I cannot do

anything to save my wife. Please do not, do not touch my wife I beg you."

The robber placed two guns on his head. Tony began to cry. Mama was scared to look up. She shivered on the floor.

The gang leader parted Mabel's thighs. He unzipped his pants. He covered her body with his. Tony saw the robber's eyes pop out. He instantly closed his eyes and imagined the robber penetrating his wife. Tony heard a painful growl.

The gang leader rolled off Mabel, he was bleeding and weak. Mabel had stabbed him; she stood up and kicked his balls several times. The last robber charged at Mabel with a killing look. He pointed two guns at Mabel. Tony was quick to pick up a heavy flower vase and crashed it on his head.

"Darling, are you okay?" Tony asked. She nodded and he gathered her in his arms. He kissed her forehead for a long time. They heard the Police siren.

Seated on the floor, Mama said, "Tony, now you see why you need a strong woman with you. Have you thought that while you may be away from home, Mabel will be the Commander in Chief of your home? She needs to be strong in order to guard and protect your children against harm. Imagine if Mabel had been a weak woman, in the face of today's danger. What do you think would be our fate by now?"

Tony held Mabel more tightly as if he was pouring his strength into her.

Twenty

The Invalid Citizen

To control the oil potentials of Kalahari, the Government forcefully dispossessed people of their lands, stripping communities of the right to claim benefits of their soil. The people's strength was no match for these invaders, their little confrontational effort led to many deaths and resulted to high percentage of casualties. The Government chiselled and drilled the belly of the soil.

The people allayed fears with hope that the exploration might not be successful. The drill was efficacious. The Government found crude oil on the soil of Kalahari. Thereon, the activities poisoned the community food systems; health and mental structure were threatened. The Government quest to control the natural resources led to degradation and devaluation of a people. This exploration polluted rivers and atmosphere; it mowed mountains and chopped down forest.

Kahiri and other indigenous people mourned the degrading status of the community. She lifted a bucket of water off her son's head. Fanny raised his shirt to clean his wet face. His tummy was very flat. He was evidently hungry.

Kahiri dusted her hands, "the water is not pure." She said and swam her hand in the water.

"The river is greasy. The sun did not set to power the solar system. It has been rainy for days. We cannot pump water. The tap is dry like wilderness," Fanny said.

Kahiri gave him an awry look, "how can I use such water to cook?"

"Mama, we do not have a choice." He checked the level of water in a black drum. "We will manage this water in the drum for drinking water," he pulled off his shirt and hung it to dry, "I will set the fire." He walked into the outdoor kitchen and brought out some firewood. He poured kerosene on the firewood and lit it.

Kahiri added sawdust to the burning firewood. The fire ignited the more. She sat on a low stool to wash a small basket of fishes. She traded smoked fishes for livelihood. The fisher folks had seen worse days in farming after oil discovery in their territory. She placed the fishes on the grill. When the fishes were properly roasted, Kahiri and her children ate two fishes with a bowl of garri.

Oakboro entered the compound. He sat on a local stretcher chair and rested his back. Kahiri picked up his cutlass and hoe. She put them away in the kitchen.

"How did work go today?" Kahiri asked. She handed him half a cup of water. He drank the water, gurgled some in his mouth, and poured out the water. Kahiri was not happy he wasted the water. She took the cup and went back to drying the fishes.

"The chemicals are ruining our farms," Oakboro said. Kahiri washed and wiped her hands on an old clean towel. She went to sit by her husband. "No matter how they try to convince us, those chemical do not give greater yield."

Kahiri sighed deeply. "Today, something peppery splashed into my eyes. I was in the middle of the river fishing. I was scared of using the oily water to wash my eyes."

"How were you able to see?"

"I licked a pinch of salt. Our fishes are dying, the chemical from the land washes into the river. In the next few days, we might not have a cup of clean water to drink. Gas inflation pollutes our air; our water and land are contaminated. I feel what is left, is the degradation of our souls with hunger bedevilling our bodies. Look at our children," he observed the little children playing, "our children look like skeletons. I could see their intestines shrinking. I could count our children's ribs."

"I was not able to harvest the crops. From tomorrow, they will have food to eat, a good meal. My waist hurts. Get some ointment. I need a massage, please."

Kahiri nodded and went into the house. Since the discovery of oil, there had been gradual increase of protracted illnesses and other diseases. The clinics were devoid of medical supplies-from standard equipment to drugs. The herbs the people once relied on for healing; the land pollution had weakened its powers and stunted its growth. Plants were dying. Human, animal, and plant cells were getting impaired. Several productions of inventive proteins caused severe health complications. The people also suffered birth defects diseases.

In the morning, Oakboro whistled as he strolled to the farm. There were deep holes and patches on the land. On seeing the state of his farmland, he held his chest and fell to the ground. Seasons of his hard work had gone down the drain. Some people found him by the bush path. They carried him home. He had had a heart attack.

Kahiri tended her husband. She bathed and massaged his body, "They are destroying agriculture in our community. They have destroyed our crops. It is now futile to go fishing. The gas exploration is destroying our fishes. Now you have fallen ill. How will I manage the household?" She fed him some herbal medicine in muffled tears.

Kahiri and Oakboro no longer had a source of livelihood. Fanny passed his Senior School Certificate Examination. She did not have the courage to tell him he will not be able to sit for JAMB.

Fanny excitedly ran into the compound, "Mama, mama! I have been awarded a scholarship to study abroad." He held the letter in tight fist. Kahiri dropped to the ground and prayed for this miraculous breakthrough. Oakboro cried. Tears rolled down his cheeks. Fanny flashed the paper in his father's face. Oakboro's tears intensified. Kahiri hugged Fanny. The younger children danced around them.

"Oakboro, it seems this is the compensation for all the wreckages," she looked at Fanny, "did they give scholarships to your classmates?"

"No Mama, I have the scholarship because I scored one of the best results in the State."

"God bless you my son. You shall be a light and share with other children of this community. Fanny, when will you be going to school?"

"Mama, I will leave in a month's time."

"Okay, I will get you some provisions."

"Don't bother Mama; the Government will pay for everything. We do not have to worry over any provisions."

"No matter what, I will give my child some provisions. I will break some kernel and collect garri-cassava flour from our neighbour. She still owes me money for the last fishes we supplied to her restaurant."

"Thank you, Mama. I am happy," Fanny hugged his mother. He touched his father's feet and placed both hands on his chest.

"They can take away our fishing ground if this education can come to all our children. Education is valuable. It makes our children gold and diamond. Great educational opportunities are a great asset. We do not mind the degradation of our land. Education is valuable, it is worth more than gold," Kahiri rejoiced.

✽ ✽ ✽ ✽ ✽ ✽

A week later, Fanny went to America to study. He sent letters home. His family was happy he was doing well.

Over the years, there was national economic crisis. There was division of resource planning. The price of crude oil dropped because the countries that depended on the product had invented substitute mechanisms and substances that served the same purpose.

There was hunger, strive and lack of peace. The people could not act on the exploitation of weak ecosystems, despoliation of ecology, destruction of power relations between the oil block owners of the resource and their exploiters.

Most people could not go back to farming because the lands were impaired. There was hunger, strife, and diseases. Kalahari looked like a glorified shanty. Despite the wealth extracted from the land, the communities lacked good infrastructures.

Kahiri's kids and other children walked through rivers to attain formal education. They reached school in wet uniforms, shivering and learning. Soon, the schools were without attendants. Many children fell ill and died from diseases. Some of the children had chopped toes caused by unknown disease due to chemical reactions.

✻ ✻ ✻ ✻ ✻ ✻

Three years later, Fanny returned from America. The Government could no longer sponsor his education. "Mama, I, and other Nigerian students tried to further our studies. We really tried. We took up menial jobs but the tuition was just too exorbitant. Some of us took to prostitution, robbery, and I was deported for trafficking drugs," Fanny could not look at his mother's face after he uttered the last statement.

"I am glad you came back home, we are happy you came back home. Your father will be glad to see you. He grows weaker every day. I am glad you are home. My son, you have grown into a handsome young man." She spanned his bulging shoulder. Fanny's beard was full and unkempt. He rubbed his rough chin on his mother's blistered palm.

"Mama, you have toiled for so many years without results. I am sorry I could not fulfil anything."

"I am just happy you are home in one piece. It gives me peace. We will go to work tomorrow. We were able to grow some crops. There is a piece of land we now farm on."

"I will not return to the farm. It is obvious we are politically not valid. We are the Invalid Citizens. The Government mistreated us because they did not find worth in our personalities and the territory we come from. They have poisoned our rivers and our soils are infertile.

Why should I go and toil on a land that can barely yield fruits? They found wealth on our lands, use it extremely to enrich government institutions and leave us to wallow in life-threatening conditions. We are the worthless people that do not deserve good standard of living and viable social amenities.

Mama, enough is enough. Our communities will no longer allow seismic drilling test that destroys our peace and sources of livelihood. They are destroying us. They have poisoned our rivers and our soils are infertile.

Mama, the soil is not fertile; the labour to make it birth crops is horrendously painstaking. I am not ready to go through such emotional and physical trauma. Our land is in shambles while the crude suckers deck their mansion with golden furniture.

They eat fresh foods, drink pure water, and breathe fresh air while we inhale foul air, drink poisoned water, and barely have food to eat. Mama, I will not return to the farm."

"What will you do if you can't work on the farm? What do you want to do? Tell me what you intend to do."

Fanny's face was marked with rage, "I will take back what belongs to me. I and other downtrodden citizens of this community will take up arm to fight the harm done to us."

Twenty — One

Highway Christmas

Deji looked forward to having a swell Christmas Holiday. He clicked on the website of Nigeria's first airline, rated best in the country. He knew Arrow Airline was a bad choice but he booked the ticket with faith they had improved services and delivery. He filled his details and payment was successful. At least, this was one time he did not have difficulty in booking ticket on their website. He relaxed for a while. Afterwards, he played music from his phone and packed a bag.

In the Davis residence, Damilola and her daughter, Yinka were arguing over an imminent trip. "If not for your silliness, we should have been in the village by now. I do not know where you picked up the habit of telling lies," Damilola said.

Mr Davis entered the living room and Yinka ran to him, "Daddy, please let me stay with you for the Christmas. I will not go to the village. I want to celebrate Christmas in the city."

"No you won't. As your mother had said, your lies delayed the trip. So no more excuses. Your school never asked you and your classmates to wait for any brochure. I do not know why we did not call your school

Principal to confirm that information. We trusted our daughter too much. You disappointed me, my dear."

"Please daddy, I am so sorry. I only wanted to stay back and celebrate Christmas with you."

"There is no need for you to stay here. Your father would be busy with work. He is travelling tomorrow as well for a two days conference. Who will look after you? Besides, he will join us on or before New Year's Eve. Yinka, I do not want to do anything irrational. Get upstairs and get your suitcases ready."

Yinka looked at her father, who she could always sweet-talk to do her bidding, "daddy, please. I will bake a cake for you. I have learned to make some delicious pastries from the recipe book you bought for me."

Mr Davis remained aloof, "Yinka, I have had enough of your whining. Go upstairs to your room and pack you and your siblings' suitcases."

"I have packed their bags." Yinka obstinately said.

"And yours?" Mr Davis asked.

"Daddy, I do not want to go to the village. I want to spend my Christmas here at home."

"Get upstairs to your room. With or without your suitcases, you will be on that plane to Akure. I am sure you do not want to leave your toiletries behind."

Yinka took one last look at her father. She kicked a chair and angrily bounded up the stairs. The couple looked exasperated. They heard their little baby crying. Mr Davis made for the stairs but his wife stopped him. "I will check on her, please confirm our flight schedule. I think the flight is for 9 am." Damilola said and went upstairs.

The harmathan weather condition was very hazy. Arrow Airline cancelled many flights because there was no possibility to fly. The passengers expressed their disappointment in various degrees. Damilola struggled with two toddlers and tried to hold her falling wig. Yinka walked behind them like a lone stranger. She was angry to leave the city.

Damilola's money fell on the floor and a strong breeze blew it away. She ran after the paper note with the speed a plane ran before takeoff. She smartly trapped the money with her feet, picked it up, and inserted it between her tight cleavages. Yinka stared at her mother in astonishment and went to stand with her siblings.

"Madam, you should not keep money that way to avoid germs," Deji said.

"Can you mind your damn business?" Damilola asked.

"Lady, I am just giving you a good advice. You could contact germs by doing that," said Deji. Damilola coldly ignored him and went to join her children.

"Mom, how could you run after Five Hundred Naira note like that? Shouldn't you have rather let it go?" Yinka asked.

"What do you know? By the time you start earning money, you will know how valuable a kobo is. Hold your siblings' hands." Yinka hesitated. "Yinka, I don't have time for your nonsense."

"Yes, grumpy mom," Yinka mumbled.

The Aircrew made their way from the airstrip. "Your airline is ridiculous. You have disappointed me so many times and often I come back to board your stupid airplanes. I am worried why I still trust your airline to take me to my destinations. I do not know where I should go from here with these kids clogging my footsteps," Damilola said.

The Aircrew walked on. They did not spare a glance at the disgruntled Passengers. Damilola patted the wailing baby in the stroller with one hand and used the other to make a call. A glint came into Yinka's eyes that they might be heading back home.

Deji dragged his bag and another cargo bag containing hose out of the airstrip. He was travelling with two bags because he had sent most of his baggage and other 'abroad items' through a friend's private car to their village. The harmathan breeze wisped his face.

The last time he came back from the United States for a vacation, he looked forward to a great family reunion. It turned out the plane could not land in the airport. There was no power supply to light up the runway. They had to fly back to Lagos where most stranded passengers slept on the floor and luggage.

He had to be in the village before Christmas Eve. He had only one option, which was travelling by road. He hated going through the hassles of road trip. The bad roads and discomforting transport system exasperated his mind even before he set out on the journey. He enquired about the best transport company in the park, and a bread seller pointed at BESS Motors.

Deji paid for the full back seat of the bus. His mind screamed comfort when he stretched his legs to relax in the air-conditioned bus. He had told the driver he wanted to rest before other passengers filled the bus. The Driver put on the air condition after Deji paid a little extra for the favour.

Deji had barely closed his eyes when he heard the door open. More passengers had booked seats. He was glad, the bus will move on soon. Damilola entered with the kids, Yinka sat on the number two seat of the bus. It was three persons to a seat and Damilola paid for a seat in the middle row.

"Madam, you will inconvenience me. Why did you not buy two seats so that you and your children will seat in comfort. How are we going to manage? The space is not a living room in a mansion. It is very tight." Her seat partner said. She gestured at Deji, "Why don't you ask him for help? He has enough space."

Damilola turned to Deji and smiled, "Please sir, can one of my children join you at the back?" Deji shook his head in disagreement. He did not want any intrusion. The space could not fit his long legs so he had to stretch his legs on the seat. Other passengers joined to plead on Damilola's behalf.

"Please sir, help me out. I don't have enough money to buy two tickets."

"Isn't the teenage girl in the front seat your daughter? You should have paid for two seats on this row and your family would have managed the space anyhow." Deji said.

"Oh, Yinka," She pointed at her daughter who already had a headphone on, "she is angry for some reasons and decided to be on her own. I just want to let her be for a while."

"And it is convenient for you to discomfort a total stranger?"

"You are not a total stranger. We met at the airport."

"Yeah we did. And you were very friendly," Damilola was embarrassed. "I don't know why I should listen to you."

"Please sir," Damilola glumly said.

Deji could not overlook Damilola's predicament. "Okay, the two toddlers can come to my seat." He shifted for the two children to come through. They playfully bounded on the narrow passage and sat with impish smiles.

"Thank you so much. God bless you." Damilola sat and sighed deeply. She made cereals for the baby and fed her.

The girl playfully pinched her brother's ear. Deji raised an eyebrow at her. She gave him a toothed grin and curt nod.

Deji winked, "What is your name, pretty girl?" He asked.

"My name is Nike, sir."

"Good girl. Settle down kids, you do not want uncle to get upset with some tantrums. If you trouble me, I will send the two of you over to your mother's seat. Is that clear?" They bobbed, "good kids." Deji smiled and relaxed his back.

Nike jammed her hand into her mouth and sucked. "Nike, will you stop that?" Damilola gave her a threatening look and made a gesticulation of slicing her fingers. Fear welled in Nike's eyes. She was quick to stop before her mother spanked her. One of her fingers had gotten a cut in the past. Damilola had tried to stop Nike from sucking. One method was nipping the thumb she suckled the most.

The company's Mechanical Engineer checked the vehicle. This was a normal routine before any motorists embarked on a journey. The Manager came out, "Driver, please drive with care."

The Driver's lips twisted in slight irritation, "I am a trusted driver of this company."

"I know BESS Motors does not have reckless drivers. However, be patient and cautious while driving. Our radar is on you; obey the company's speed limit. This is Christmas Eve. Safely drive them to their destination to enjoy the festivities."

"I will, sir." The Driver said.

"Merry Christmas everyone!" The Manager said. The Passengers called out good wishes as the vehicle moved. The Driver turned on the radio to listen to the morning news. Afterwards, songs started playing.

Some of Deji's favourite songs played on the radio. He nodded with satisfaction to the beats. "This is amazing. Cool music. We are in smooth hands." Deji relaxed. He stretched his legs as best as he could.

THE INVALID CITIZEN AND OTHER STORIES

Most residents of the city were travelling to spend Christmas in their hometowns. The Driver hooted the car horn for a truck pusher to get out of the way. The road was congested. There was a lot of traffic. It took a long time before the vehicle began to speed.

Deji was uncomfortable, "the price I paid for the whole back seat is a waste," he muttered.

Nike wanted a larger cut of chocolate and her older brother gave her a small portion. A fight ensued between siblings. Deji tried to separate them but he could not keep the toddlers at bay for long.

To maintain peace and order, Damilola had to transfer to the back seat while her son took her seat. Nike fell asleep. She snuggled deeper into her mother's thighs. It was difficult for Damilola to hold her suckling baby.

Deji brushed two strands of Nike's braids aside. Her eyebrows were a perfect carve. He smiled when the child laughed mildly in her sleep.

Damilola extended a hand to Deji, "my name is Damilola Davis."

Deji shook her hand, "I am Deji Cole. I am pleased to meet you."

"Do you have kids?" The question surprised Deji. She gave him a warm smile that urged him to answer.

Deji looked straight-faced, "no, I do not. My wife, she is not ready to have kids. She is an American. I just got back from the States. We are based in Los Angeles," Deji stared at Nike.

"Oh, I see, typical. She is conscious of gaining weight I guess. I understand. I was a beauty queen, and now this," she glanced at her plump body.

"Motherhood changes the woman's body. Bearing children is a generous phase of a woman's life. Believe me when I say you must be looking more beautiful than you were. It is not all my wife's decision. I am not good with having kids around. But I wanted us to try. She is in the peak of her dancing career and I do not want to kill her passion or cause any distraction with insisting we start having kids."

"I understand your plight." Damilola nodded.
"Yeah," Deji said.

"So tell me. Have you come home to take a Nigerian wife that will bear children?"

"My mother has already married one for me. I will not accept it. I did not want to come home because of my mother's deed. I am going to see my father who is recovering from a surgery and give a present to a friend."

"Oh, I am sorry to hear that. I wish your father a quick recovery and a Merry Christmas. I wish you the best in convincing your mother. Most mothers cannot do without meddling in their children's issues. She is just a mother concerned about her son."

"That is her business. I am a grown man. I will not accept that woman. I am legally married. I love my wife so much."

The baby's toe nudged Nike's eyes. She yelled and started crying. Damilola became confused between which children to first console.

Deji asked Damilola to pass the little baby to him. He rocked the baby gently and crooned soothing words. She admired his devotion.

Deji luxuriated in the feeling. It was the first time he had ever held a baby this close. The emotion of having his own baby seized him. She noticed and prayed for his wish to come true.

They got to Ore, a busy suburb of Ondo State with many eateries and local relaxation spots for travellers. The road was a death trap. It was full of parked tankers and potholes. The increasing rate of accidents along the highway made many travellers weary.

Travellers who could not afford better means of transportation embarked on road trips with fervent prayers. Speeding and reckless driving was the order of the day on the expressway. The results of these bad road situations were deaths and casualties.

There was over congestion in the morgues around the highway and it had many unclaimed corpses. As the vehicle slowed down for a mourning crowd, doctors in black robes came into view. The Managements of some morgues were carrying out a mass burial for unclaimed corpses that were road accident victims.

Suddenly, there was a roaring fire from across the road. There had been an explosion. A fuel station had exploded. The deafening scream of Damilola and her children jostled Deji awake. The inferno was raging. Few passers-by scurried to get away from its glowing claws.

The flame was monstrous. There was a prison yard close to the fuel station. Some wardens rushed out in fright. The Prison Director evacuated the prisoners and commanded them to form a chain and they were ushered to a safe side of a bush to sit on the ground.

Motorists and passengers were terrified. Drivers marched hard on brakes to drive backward, fleeing from the chaos. The roaring fire drowned screams and cries for help. Some passengers in buses that was close to the fuel station alighted and skittered across the road.

The fire was breaking out fast. BESS bus was on the other side of the road. Deji asked the Driver to stop the bus but he refused, "you will put us all in danger. I must get us to safety. Everyone, buckle your seat belts tighter," the Driver said.

Deji gritted his teeth in anger. "I am not asking for all of you to get down. Driver, stop the vehicle. I need to get down, alone."

"No sir, it is my duty to get you safe to your destination," he increased his driving speed. The tracker began to beep. BESS Motors stopped the vehicle movement. He called the office to explain the situation. Before he ended the call, Deji had opened the door and gotten out. Deji took the cargo bag from the boot.

The Driver hung the call. He rushed towards Deji and held the bag. Deji punched him on the shoulder and pushed him out of his way, "to hell with you. I have to lend a helping hand in this situation. There is a mad fire out there. Are you blind to see or what? Open your eyes, man. And get out of my way!" The Driver held Deji's waist in an effort to drag him into the bus. Deji shoved him with an elbow. He held his abdomen and winced at the sharp pain.

There was a river nearby. Deji unzipped the cargo bag and rolled out a very long double hose into the water. He got a machine from a Tube

THE INVALID CITIZEN AND OTHER STORIES

Doctor, fixed the hose to it, and started the engine. He hauled it over the road. The Driver and other people watched in amazement.

Damilola got off the vehicle. "Madam, where are you going? No, you cannot do this, please get back inside," the Driver said and spread his arms to block her. She thrust her baby in his arms before he could utter another word of '*getting them to safety*.'

"Oh, I will surely lose my job," the Driver lamented while he craned the baby on his shoulder and rocked her.

Damilola ran to assist Deji. The chain-gang prisoners saw their struggle and joined them to haul the heavy hose. They hauled it and stood at a safe distance from the fire. Deji switched on the control and water gushed out, spraying the monstrous firestorm.

The fire squealed for a long while and died to a smoke. A two-hose siphoning was a great way to put out the fire. People cheered the heroes with whistles and applause. The fire service vehicle blared it siren, announcing its untimely arrival. Deji was happy the hose came in handy on the highway. He had bought it as a gift for a friend who owned a drilling and dredging company.

The victims were the occupants in the fuel station. There was gnashing of teeth and tears as the burnt bodies became visible. The scare had thrown the road upside down. In trying to turn, some trailers fell and blocked the highway. There was no way for tolling vans to come through in order to lift the fallen vehicles. Night fell.

The motorists and travellers got tired of muttering over the helpless situation. Slowly, the highway turned into a daylight hub due various traders' lamps lit to illuminate their wares. Many passengers were with little or no cash and needed to buy edibles, toiletries and other attractive items. The Tube Doctor stood as the cashier for sales men and women. Buyers transferred payment to his bank account for goods purchased. The honest Tube Doctor would withdraw the money and give to the traders on fee charges for his services.

Police officers mounted roadblocks for more security measures. When some prison wardens were unsuspecting, one of the deadly prisoners was able to break his chain. He ran into the bush. His face glowed as he skirted through the bush to freedom.

Damilola and her younger children fed from a plate of roasted plantains and fish while Deji assisted to feed the little baby from a bottle.

Yinka stopped picking at the chopped plantains. She looked sad. "So we will not get to celebrate a decent Christmas," she said.

Nike made a sad face too and stopped eating. Their disappointment unsettled Deji. He wished he could brighten the children's faces with a memorable Christmas.

"I wish daddy was here with us. My daddy always knows how to make things all right. Mom, you really should have allowed me stay back in Lagos with dad. I told you I did not want to spend Christmas in the village. You did not listen to me. I should not be here at this godforsaken place at this time. I cannot blow firecrackers with my friends in the city. Now, this incident deprives me of having a decent Christmas Eve at the village." Yinka threw the food away and went to stand close to the debris of the fire incident.

Her brother sulked and ate slowly. Damilola was disturbed. She stopped eating and pushed the food away. Deji gave her a reassuring look and passed the baby to her.

Yinka wandered into the bush. She saw a rabbit. She looked backward and saw people about different activities. She ran after it in excitement. She marvelled at the serenity and green lives that abound in the forest. She spread her arms like a bird and flapped, imagining her appearance atop a tree. She gave up the silly gimmick and resumed running.

As Yinka ran in slow motion, she tried to mimic the chirping sounds of the birds and laughed at her failed attempt. She stopped chasing when everywhere grew dark. She was far from light.

On the radio, rave of the moment was a lion had gone missing. The zoo was close to the highway. There was uproar. Families started keeping one another close. Damilola gathered her baby in a protective hug. Deji held the toddlers.

She looked around in shock, "where is Yinka? Has anyone seen my daughter?" her question echoed in the frenzy atmosphere, "has anyone seen my baby around? Someone answer me, please." She turned around and Deji tried to calm her.

Everybody was busy getting to the safety of vehicles and houses. The villagers allowed the strangers into their homes and securely closed the doors.

"Get the children into the vehicle, I will search for Yinka," Deji handed the toddlers to her. Damilola was hesitant, "go, I will bring Yinka to you."

"Promise me you will bring my daughter to me, please."

"I promise," Deji confidently said. She nodded and hastened to the vehicle with the children. Deji turned around, frantically calling out to Yinka.

Yinka had become scared. She could not find her way out of the forest. She sat hunched under a gigantic tree, "Mommy, I am scared. Oh, Lord, please light my way so that I can get out of this forest." She cried. A lion roared. Yinka cringed and fell to the ground, "God, I am going to die. Oh, I do not want to be away from my family. Tomorrow is Christmas. Save me, Lord Jesus." The lion roared recurrently and Yinka shivered fearfully in the cold night.

The lion's roar sent chills down peoples' spines. Damilola was very worried. She cried and prayed silently for her daughter's safety. Deji was yet to find any lead to Yinka's whereabouts. Nobody was willing to stop and hear out the description of a missing teenage girl.

A hunter stopped to pay heed, "yes, I saw a girl like that. I thought she was only going to ease herself and get back to her parents. Where could she be? I doubt if she had gone beyond the sides of the bush. I had seen her standing by the bush."

"Please, help me out. You know this forest well. Help me to find the child." The Hunter nodded and they went into the bush with hopeful thoughts of finding Yinka.

The lion found Yinka. It stuck out salivating tongue on seeing a fresh meal in less than two hours out of captivity. Yinka crunched backwards. She was sweating and saying prayers. She closed her eyes, waiting for the worse. Tears dropped down Yinka's cheeks. She wished she had not gotten angry and spoken rudely to her mother and then walked away, "I am sorry mommy."

The lion leisurely pranced around Yinka as if waiting for her to say her last prayers. Yinka opened her eyes because death had not come to her. At that moment, the lanky lion charged at her. Yinka's throat was too sour to scream. She balled her body and waited for death. She heard a loud scream and a heavy thud. The lion fell on the ground. The Prisoner lifted a spear and rammed it into the lion's heart. The wild beast writhed and died.

The Prisoner came to Yinka and stretched a hand. Yinka moved backwards, "do not turn away from me, I am here to help," She looked at the spear. The Prisoner dropped the bloodied weapon, "come with me. I will take you to your parents." Yinka stood up and fell down. She had sprained her left ankle somehow. The Prisoner lifted Yinka on his back. He made his way out of the bush.

The Prisoner reached the highway. Yinka had fallen asleep. Deji and the Hunter saw them by the bush. In a flash, Deji was all over Yinka. He checked her pulse and body for injury, "She is all right. I found her in the bush. I killed the lion before it got to her. You will need to check her ankle." The Prisoner said.

"Thank you so much sir, you just saved a mother from heart attack." Deji carried Yinka to her crying mother.

The Prisoner looked back at the bush. He made his way to the chained gang and took his spot. He shackled his ankles. He was content he was able to save a soul. For once in his life, he was at the right place to do a kind deed. He opened the locket around his neck and looked at his family he lost in a robbery attack that he had masterminded. The smile on his wife and children's eyes seemed to be telling him *good job!*

Inside the vehicle, Damilola said to her daughter, "Do not ever get out of my sight like that."

"Never will I do such a thing, mom. I am sorry for my earlier outburst. Anywhere with you is the best moment ever." Emotions got the better of mother and child. They hugged, teary eyed.

"So, what next?" Deji asked himself. He knew Yinka would still record this as her most boring Christmas ever. The lion's near attack traumatized Yinka. This was going to be an uncomfortable Christmas. A glint came into Deji's eyes. *There should not be a boring moment with Deji!* He thought.

Deji approached and spoke to the Tube Doctor who shook his head at what he told him. In turn, the Tube Doctor whispered to a young man who ran away to the closest homestead. Few minutes later, there was a clang of gong. Many indigenes began to emerge from their homes.

A thick bush was set on fire. The highway became a glowing dawn. Deji and some young men cut down a tree. They shaped it to a gigantic Christmas tree. Some travellers brought out their Christmas tree ornaments. Some women and children decorated from below, while Deji and some men used ladders to attend top of the tree.

Some men set-up grills. Ten minutes later, there were meat and fish barbecue sizzling on the grill. The closest eatery made food deliveries with bikes and bicycles. Music jammed from various car stereos. The prison wardens allowed the prisoners join the celebration. Their chains formed a rhythmic music as they sang '*by the rivers of Babylon.*'

When it was twelve o'clock, all and sundry shouted, *Merry Christmas!* The Driver of BESS Motors smiled and increased the volume of his stereo. He danced unreservedly and ate a big morsel of fish.

A text message came to Deji's phone. It was from his wife. The message read '*I am pregnant! Darling, we are going to be parents. You will be a father soon!*'

Deji was excited. He requested someone to play, 'On the First day of Christmas my true love gave to me!' He held the children' hands, they formed a big circle and danced around the Christmas tree. Yinka joyfully danced with her mother.

www.ingramcontent.com/pod-product-compliance
Lightning Source LLC
Chambersburg PA
CBHW021918170626
46807CB00007B/2883